WHAT WE
LEAVE BEHIND

Dave Haywood

Fisher King Publishing

WHAT WE LEAVE BEHIND

Published by
Fisher King Publishing

fisherkingpublishing.co.uk

Back cover image of blood courtesy of Vecteezy.com

To Rebecca and Riley.
My world.

And, to my Dad. He didn't get to see this book in print but I know he was over the moon that I'm going to be a proper author.

Miss you Dad.
Hope this makes you proud.

Acknowledgements

I never thought I would be dedicating a real book that I have written to anyone. I've given them as gifts aplenty to the serial bookworms and dragons in my family. (My mum loves a 'Lee Childs,' every Christmas). But dedicating one? That's major.

I should probably let you know how this ride began, so deep breath, here we go.

As some of you know I work for the Metropolitan Police as a PCSO. (Police staff for reference). I'm not a PC or anything like that, but joined as PCSO because I love the community engagement side of the job.

This brought my career into the path of the then Borough Commander, Steve Wallace, who saw me tip-tapping away at a computer and asked the question;

"Are you good on computers then?"

From there, I helped with social media and started telling the stories of policing life, which brought a problem to my screen.

Media law prohibited me from saying certain things so I had to fill in to get the engagement. I employed everything from dad jokes and puns to dramatic writing, which worked, and we quickly gained a global following. Crime prevention advice is universal.

Then the comments started.

'You should write a book!'

Spoiler alert. You're reading it.

And now the dedications.

Obviously, family comes first, so a massive thank you

to them all for being utter legends and listening to this excited puppy tell the tales I was planning. Couldn't have done it without you!

Then the strangers who graced my presence. I spoke to authors and agents, publishers and people all wanting me to succeed, and while the list below is not extensive, these few changed my life.

To Sarah. You got me to Fisher King's door. Literally wouldn't be here if you hadn't sent that email. You changed my life and I am forever thankful.

To Jo, Jojo, and Mich. You were my test audience and gave me the strength, through my doubt to get this bloody thing finished. You're amazing and awesome and other words meaning excellent. And yes, I am working on the next one we spoke of.

To Niki who helped me save a cat.

To my gaming group, the Heroes and Halfwits who followed their noble leader Zinrie through the fire to get this published.

And finally, to the too many to mention followers of my pages. I hope you like this. It's a chunk of my writing in the format you love. Let me know what you think! But I will mention one person, (not by name) who I met at a low point and talked to for a long while. Keep going. You've got this. I'll sign one for you.

Thank you all for the support.

I feel we are all on this ride together now. You made this happen!

Please enjoy PC Alex Chambers.

And welcome to my world.

Prologue

All things meet at some point in their lifespan. Atoms always collide. Musical notes join to form everything from a repetitious song to the rising heights of a symphony.

Hearts will take the chance to entwine. Children become amalgams of their parents, hopefully taking the best aspects of them both and leaving the worst behind. They move through life's journey, learning like sponges until they become the people nature and nurture decree.

Then the learning becomes harder as life brings change, brings pain, and steals love away. It tests the normally still waters of a person's mental health to see how those ripples affect actions.

Those innocent children fight to grow and push through life's viciousness; they either survive, thrive or burn in agony. And those flames sometimes engulf others, the heat of chaos searing pain into lifelines. The lick of flame reaches out to touch others, to cause the anguish it intends.

All things meet at some point.

In time. In blood. In death.

Where things truly begin is the question though, because beginnings can be from actions, from consequences. A missed call or an errant, distracted glance can change a person's direction forevermore.

But where to start? With my story? Or theirs? Hers?

Do we begin where it ends? Where I end?

We should though, as it always seems to, start with the rain.

Chapter One

Rob looked out of the window at the long shadows of the dark morning. The sun had not bothered to drag itself up as early as the forty-year-old man who searched for its light had done. It was difficult enough having to travel into the city without the grimness of the winter morning adding to his already sour mood. The warm rays of the sun were urgently needed by all commuters as it was incredibly depressing leaving and returning home from work in pitch darkness.

And whilst October was not winter cold as yet, a little heat would ease the muscles and brighten outlooks.

'The train waits for no man,' Rob reminded himself and made a mental note of whereabouts to stand on the Bournemouth Station platform so that his exit through Waterloo station was as expeditious as possible.

He hated London but that's where the real banking money was. His aspiration of running one of the lesser-known, but highly prestigious chains was his ultimate goal, but currently, the Midland Bank on the Strand would have to suffice.

"Fuck." He verbally corrected himself as his company had recently been bought outright by the Hong Kong and Shanghai Banking Corporation, or HSBC for short. He'd never get used to it. He'd been in the branch from college, working his way up the ranks. But now, as assistant manager, he had been waiting for the incumbent branch manager to die for years so that he could ultimately step into his shoes.

The walk to the station brought with it the first few drops of rain and each watery impact, though tiny, seemed to push his shoulders down. He finally made it to the shelter of the covered station and at this hellish hour, the concrete waiting area was all but empty. One jacketed figure sat huddled on one of the last wooden seats but was shrouded in darkness as the strip light above him was broken.

"Bloody drunk tourists," Rob said out loud with some venom, but not with enough volume that the figure could hear.

Turning, he went back to his chosen spot, which he used every weekday morning. Looking down at his feet, he took two side steps to his right so that he was in perfect position to open the handle of the slam door carriage. He stepped forward into the now showering rain as the train aimed for the furthest end of the platform.

It would be a brief moment in the downpour as carriages flashed by him.

The force of the hands at his back was so unexpected that Rob fell forward onto the side of the slowing train.

Had it been going faster, he might have been rebounded back onto the safety of the platform with lesser injuries, but he fell, dragged down, and into the metallic grinder of the undercarriage.

Chapter Two

Gerald sat staring out of the window most days. He couldn't remember first sitting down. Couldn't even remember where the window led to. It was obviously to the outside, but where though? He didn't know that either. His condition left him with blanks, missing time, and thoughts long forgotten.

The chair seemed as old as the frail man sitting there, staring into the murky depths of the poorly maintained garden beyond the pane of glass. They weren't lucky enough to have double glazing here, but the wooden framed windows were maintained at least.

Gerald shifted his aching bones as he thought about the day behind him. He tried to remember simple things, such as the last thing he ate, but recalling simple things was almost an impossibility. He couldn't even remember the sunlight of the previous morning.

Each day blurred into the next and he couldn't place a difference in the days he lived. 'Lived,' wasn't accurate in any way shape or form though. Existed? No. He was simply just 'there'.

On a day like today, the old man hoped for sunshine, and to be whisked away from this drab room to a beach where waves washed the sand flat, and all sins were swept into the ocean. Never to be seen again.

But all he could do was move uncomfortably as his broken body ached in disagreement with the flat lifeless cushion beneath him. Everything now ached to the point of pain.

The nurses were lovely, and they were especially

affectionate toward him, although he couldn't recall a name until they came to assist with a basic need, reaching down to brush crumbs away or help with movement. The only thing he made sure to do himself was to wash and even that most basic of skill was daunting. But he vowed that he would not allow himself to sink so low as to have to be sponge bathed, and his body still allowed him that meagre amenity.

He had reasons to conceal himself from others too.

The nurses had promised to bring him his favourite special strawberry jelly today but it hadn't arrived.

'Another broken vow,' he mused annoyedly. 'Why was it always raining as well? Every single day,' Gerald moaned internally. Constant pouring, constant drizzle, constant storms. There was never a flood though which was strange with the sheer amount of volume of water drenching everything in its path.

'People should be getting about in boats, not those infernal automobiles,' he said, unsure if it was internally or externally vocalised. To the outside world though, Gerald had not uttered a word since moving into the retirement home years before. He had come to Shady Oaks Residential Care Home through the local council, housed there with his single suitcase. Partially funded by them and his last cash reserves, he was placed there until he would die, the dictionary definition of God's waiting room.

And with Gerald well into the latter stage of his life, the council and care home thought it would not be for very long. His last birthday sealed his 80th year.

No one came with presents. No cake was delivered.

The nurses sang the traditional birthday song, but also a second one, which was a lovely treat for the elderly man and somehow he remembered the lyrical tones of their voices.

'Why, though?' He tried to remember. Why would he remember the melody of the song, but not what they were singing? He whistled the tune noiselessly, blowing little more than what his cheeks allowed as the rain continued its torrential attack on the world it fell on.

Moments later, everything he had remembered was now a mystery and he mulled over his new thoughts. He detested existing like this, forever forgetting, but more so he hated the living. He wished his end would come soon so that he would get a blessed release from the monotony of unmemorable days. He had nothing and no one, except the vapid nurses who treated him like a child. God, he hated them all.

The old man scanned the room, as his memory changed course once again. Other people were milling about, but none were concentrating on him. He was alone, lost to his repeating thoughts.

All he knew was that something was coming.

And he awaited the arrival.

Chapter Three

Service. The Job. A career like no other.

Running towards what most people flee.

The metaphorical, physical but often emotionally burning building was our wheelhouse, which is not a great office environment for the average layperson to be fair. What with the fire and all the 'aaarrrggghhhs'.

But someone had to do it, and it was a wage at the end of the day. It did however have an annoying habit of filling dreams and dominating days and my mind was currently check listing through yesterday's tasks whilst utterly sound asleep. Even slumbering, I would make sure that everything was covered and complete. If one thing was left or brushed aside, it could mean life or death at times. Plus, why would you do a job if not correctly?

The dream paperwork loomed and towered over my imaginary desk in this doozy of a bedtime fantasy. As in the cartoons, my desk shrunk, creaking under the weight of the groaning stack. The light in my illusionary office dwindled alongside the encroaching pillar making the imagined room feel claustrophobic. Threatening to topple, the papered pile tottered as if to throw its contents into an abyss of disarray. Even realising that I was in snoozeville, I felt crushed under the weight of work until a screeching alarm exploded in the now tiny phantasmal workspace.

The strident ring got ever louder as the enormous paperwork stack finally toppled, throwing paper, hastily jotted thoughts, and case notes, everywhere.

'I'm going to have to sort all this,' I mused sleepily as I thudded against the desk. I felt pushed from behind, and it woke me up from the anxiety nightmare that was becoming all too commonplace nowadays. Why can't I just dream of heroic unicorns with bazookas saving the world? Or go through the latest in the Marvel movies, scene by scene, you know, like normal people do.

But no. There's always the worry that work will get too much, and I'll mess things up and make mistakes. The slightest misstep could have grave consequences so the panic of oversight weighed on me like a coffin lid closing, shutting out all light and hope.

I stirred into reality, away from the initially comic dream, and quietly thanked the Lord that I didn't have to sort through all that paper. The chiming of the alarm called for my attention as the second occupant of the bed nudged me to turn off the call to awaken. I got an unwelcome dig of an elbow into my spine as I tried to find the off switch.

"Gimme a sec woman!" I playfully retorted, quietly though to not fully wake her. The elbow-spine-diggy system is not a great motivational tool, but I loved her so thought to let her off.

'This was the desk thud thing from my dream!' I realised, thinking it was quite trippy. Silence filled the bedroom and from where I lay, the grey of the clouds could be seen through the slats of the blind, which sought to dampen my mood.

"Shoo cloud, don't bother me!" I sang quietly, sticking the rhyme in my head. Even the ungodly hour would not stop me from my day's work, which started with getting a nice cuppa down me.

The woman groaned and rolled over, blissfully falling asleep again.

'Why are early shifts so gosh darn early?' I thought angrily to myself. The sun hadn't called forth a single droplet of sweat off of any overly eager runners and here I was dragging myself further toward the oncoming day. An early shift in my designated ward officer role, or DWO to be swanky, started at 07:00hrs with a team briefing and a coffee, (thank the maker), and at this hour, a dark warming brew was very much needed. It would mix well with the one I was about to have as caffeine was needed well before that meeting could, or should, take place.

No one needs a grumpy Alex before 07:05hrs. It normally took me an hour to travel to Kingston, a wonderful London community nestled in the southwest. I found great pleasure in calling it a Surrey borough though, as to particular residents, it was a geographical wind-up of epic proportions.

"Alex, you jolly well know by now, Kingston Upon Thames was absorbed into Greater London in the mid-60s," I got told this every single time I made my preplanned faux pas, the resident missing my tongue wedged firmly in my cheek.

Humour was good for morale, even if the recipient missed the playful prodding. And you especially need a chuckle in my line of work.

Flipping the kettle into life, I went and sloshed myself clean, getting some warm clothes ready for the crisp October morning. The instant coffee was just a starter for more cups to come having had a previous late one in front of the telly. I say late, but when you start this early, 20:00 hrs is like an all-nighter at the local discotheque.

Steam rose from the kettle as I shoved a chocolate hobnob into my mouth, getting crumbs in my now salt-and-pepper beard.

I'd fallen asleep numerous times trying to watch a poorly produced cold case drama Channel 5 had vomited into commission, but as I worked for the police, it was still of interest. I enjoyed trying to catch the suspect before the ending explained what 'cold case,' meant. Most of the episodes left questions hanging in that ominous trailer voice that had no intention whatsoever of answering the scallywag. You'd have to tune in next week etc etc.

Becoming a police constable in the Metropolitan Police began fifteen years ago, as I strived for more out of my life. More stories. More satisfaction. And the pension was a definite bonus too. Having always worked in sales prior to that, I found it a conversation killer at parties when the only question I ever received would be, "What do you sell?" and after the answer of (insert whatever I was selling at the time, but a boring product nonetheless) an awkward silence would fall. How do you follow that up in conversation unless you need a new air conditioning unit or a swanky fax machine? Because I never seemed to sell anything remotely sexy, it didn't get me high on the invite list. Add to that the sucky hours for sales and you had a concoction for 'postal worker loses the plot'.

But when I did eventually join the boys and girls in blue, the stories flowed. In abundance. Even though I had wedged myself firmly into the area of local neighbourhood policing, which was considered the quieter side of the job, I had still seen things. Both the good, bad, and downright weird sides of people. Residents meet police on their worst of days, being in the darkest of moods because of whatever incident had befallen them. Burglary, robbery, and assault, all happen to residents not expecting it. I mean no one wants crime to happen to them, but they never seem to expect it to happen to them. Criminals were generally good at the surprise aspect of their job, I will give them that.

But we were there to assist as best we could, to sweep up people's problems and help with reassurance. Sometimes we would crack their case, but for others, it was just simply impossible due to lack of something. (Normally people-power, but lack of evidence also scuppers cases quite often).

Then you would get the complaints coming in.

"Why didn't you solve my case that had zero evidence, no DNA, and no CCTV? You must reopen my case!"

We're good, but even Sherlock Holmes had some sort of evidence to go on. Plus the buggers in finance had not approved my deerstalker/pipe requisition. I was also not allowed one of those oversized magnifying glasses for clue hunting.

What people don't realise is an officer's every day is their worst of days. Just let that sink in for one moment. No one ever calls us and says, "I know I've called 999, but just wanted to say thanks. And the kettle's always on at 29 Acacia Road."

It can be a tough job, and we truly hate it when we can't catch the bad guy, but more so, help the victim. That's what breaks even the hardiest of heroes.

I enjoy speaking to the local communities and trying

to assist them but at almost 50, my days of working nights and blue light runs were a distant past. Safer Neighbourhoods complimented that and rapid response was very much a young man's game. In addition the years of foot patrolling had given my knees a wonderful ache and crunching crack when used. Legs seem to age quicker than any other body part in the police. These days they sounded more like a bag of castanets being thrown down a flight of stairs. Again, I chuckled at my hilarity, even though it was unfortunately all too true.

Coffee number one was warming my insides as I was dressing, so I snuffled another. Getting my train of thought choo-chooing back to getting my butt in gear, I remembered already sorting a clean uniform for the day ahead and allowed myself a smug little grin and a head wobble of complacency.

'Thank you, past me,' I praised myself. One shirt would suffice as it was fortunately not the sweltering summer months as you could easily sweat through two or even three changes of shirt as the weight of the stab vest clung onto moist pits.

"Moist..." I said out loud, chuckling to myself.

Summer's too hot. Winter's too cold and those young 'uns should pull their trousers up.

I was becoming a grumpy old man, and this morning, as life started to claw its way to Tuesday, I felt my age. I trudged my way to the bus stop, each footstep a lumbering ox not wanting to leave the safety of my lovely warm woman. Sorry, home. To top it all I felt the first few drops of rain as the clouds drew in.

"Balls."

Chapter Four

"Thanks, driver!" I chirped as I got to the stop nearest the old listed building designated as our base of operations. It was without any other departments, just a satellite station near our ward boundaries.

The heavy wooden doors bestowed their historic foreboding while the morning light yawned itself awake as I jabbed my pass code into the lock. Ironically, behind this old oaken barrier and the decorative frontage stood a modern grey office building, only exposed as a secure police area by the metallic blue Star Trek sliding doors. Ours were a lot less high-tech though, and without the efficient sound that always accompanied the captain's entrance. The building was going to be up for sale soon, as it was too costly for the Met in uncertain times of austerity.

'Better to lose buildings over bodies,' I thought, even if they had nowhere to sit, or work.

The office was cluttered with years of intelligence about the local area on whatever wall space could be used without the fire officer complaining. He was such a stickler for things like that as 'building on fire,' was his one job. That and checking the smoke alarms, which made him an honorary member of the London Fire Brigade. Just without the plumbing day job or villa in Spain.

The room housed a fridge of dubious working order which was often a foul-smelling hell hole where Tupperware goes to die, its contents bringing to life whole new ecosystems. Whenever it was rota'd to be the other team's turn to clean, it always fell to the PCSO as in their words, the 'Support' in their title meant that it was their job. I begged to differ as you should never give a job to someone that you wouldn't do yourself, and it was a bit of a knob move too.

We were also graced with a single working chair that looked down upon its broken brethren. That was the skipper's arse rest of choice and her minions all fought and struggled for the best of the rest. Yes, there was a strong feeling of chair envy in our little team.

PC Danny Morgan was always first in but never had the coffee ready. He was the newest member of the team and the most rambunctious, working hard to fast-track his way up the chain of command without a year's service to his name. How he got through training without reading the white notes on tea making and buying the correct biscuits, will forever be beyond me. Being quite gung-ho and quick to rile, his young years had not brought him much 'street sav'. It made him a boisterous little puppy with a taser, hyped up on superheroism and cans of Monster. So, in our trade that gave him the fictitious rank of 'shit magnet'.

We were a family though and I had taken him under my wing, trying to arm him with the tools he needed to succeed, and more importantly, not get killed in service by mouthing off to the wrong person. I'd seen it all before. The uniform goes on and the officer thinks he's a super person, which they most definitely aren't.

'The best bit of kit we have Dan is our mind and temperament,' I had told him sagely on more than one occasion. I wish I had one of those intellectual-looking pipes to add to the gravitas. Oh! Maybe a monocle too. This was top-shelf training, so I think the adornments were warranted. He normally 'listened,' to my helpful tips whilst swinging his cuffs around like some sort of crap cowboy, or budget stripper about to take down some particulars.

Dan was busying himself this morning with old paperwork, filing things in an affront to my repeatedly offended OCD. I called it OCD as it was better than saying 'stuck in my ways,' which felt like a reaffirmation of my old fart status. I refused to accept that I had a case of 'Old Coppers Demeanour,' and point blank rejected the term 'back in my day'. I shivered, shrugging off the age and reminding myself that I was indeed, hip AND trendy.

Papers slipped from his hands as Sergeant Jess McClaren boldly strode in. She had already bought herself a piping hot 'too many adjectives,' coffee from the posh place on the corner, without wondering if it needed to be skinny or Ariana Grande. She also didn't think to ask if I wanted one either, but she was the skipper so I wasn't going to raise it as an issue. I also had no idea what item had been milked to complete her beverage, so best avoided. Can someone please tell me where the teat is on an almond?

She was a bullish person in general, speaking her mind without thought. Not in a malicious way, just an abrupt one, as if every syllable needed to be actioned with a salute, every PowerPoint made hammered out with authority.

We team briefed and were tasked as appropriate to rank with Dan being assigned to our sister ward team to help with a warrant. They were about to open a door, quite politely, with what we affectionately called our 'big red key'. It tended to leave a mark or two when used though, which made for a great photo for the social media team. Our followers did love a criminal getting his door bashed in and getting his comeuppance comeupped. Some of the more burly officers would try and take the entire door off and out of its frame with as few hits as possible. Because man. Grrrr. I'm amazed that when CID got there, there weren't drawings of buffalo on the suspect's walls, in the obligatory Met blue biro.

I was given the less dramatic task of foot patrolling the south of our ward which luckily encompassed part of the main high street and the flavoursome temptations of the food market.

To fill out our ranks, we were waiting for a new Police Community Support Officer as the last one had retired. He was a sweet bloke but realised it was time to hang up his notebook when he couldn't remember where he put it. PCSOs are great if you get the right one, but I sometimes found myself getting jealous if they were too chatty. That was my favourite bit of neighbourhood work!

And so it was time.

Time to set out and stop crime, reassure my residents and maybe get a proper coffee of the Ariana scale. Earn my wages, burn boot leather, and don't get anyone hurt. An easy mantra that has allowed me to get another year closer to the lovely pension.

Gathering my kit, I checked that I had my standard bits and bobs but most importantly, my pocket notebook, or 'PNB,' for short. I leafed through it because if you left them lying around, some of the more Neanderthal officers would 'knob,' it. This means that if a stray PNB is found, they'll draw a massive cock on one of the empty pages. Hilarious. Although saying that, someone in response was quite arty. He would get all the veins, hair, and even some expelled errant droplets in. I even saw one with some shading in to give it its just girth.

I opened the door to the yard and a downpour, water drenching everything in sight.

"Balls."

Chapter Five

Darkness, all-encompassing.

No light, no hope.

Just the constant voices, the screaming.

The ensembled tones collected in the blackness were from both men and women and also a few children, although none were distinct enough from the other. The words uttered mixed and overlapped so sentences rolled into each other creating jumbled thoughts that were unintelligible.

All the mass felt was emotion.

They had no recollection of how long the darkness was their forced home. The voices remained a mass of shouts, of screams, crying into the void of endless time.

They couldn't find each other, to help or be helped themselves.

They were lost.

Cracks were appearing in the darkened walls of their confinement, and while no light still entered, they began to feel a form long forgotten.

Some of the voices used their raw emotional state as a focus to reach whatever the surface consisted of, clawing up to scream out their anger at their captor unseen.

The collection realised that they weren't floating in this inky prison, we were just... there.

A consciousness in chaos.

But one that was finding its voice.

Recently though, time was becoming apparent to the unnumbered within, and they began to focus on it. With each moment, they formed themselves into a collective to fight back against the hell that they were incarcerated within.

Horror gave strength, and in confusion, vengeance grew.

The voices had waited long enough.

Time was on their side.

Chapter Six

"Rain, rain go away," I muttered out loud as a burly response team driver passed. He was half my age and in it for the action as the young ones sometimes were. I stared into the yard where all the police cars awaited their drivers and controllers, to speed off heroically to call after call, saving everyone's day.

A mountainous PC approached and as he did, his size blocked all sunlight out and left me in shadow, such was his breadth. He was stuffing what was left of a bacon sandwich into the gaping maw hidden beneath a humongous, bristling ginger beard. The food disappeared as the massive sausage-fingered giant poked at the bacon-based morsel.

He looked like a Viking in police clothing and imposed over me as the remnants of the breakfast were jammed further into the depths of his facial hair. I almost warned him to remove said sausagey digits as he'd need them for driving but thought it better to question the orange-haired BFG.

He must've been a full foot taller than me, making me feel like there was a golden goose hidden somewhere in one of the custody cells. I would not like to be on the wrong end of a roll-around with this behemoth of a man, which is what I am trying to portray here. I imagined him walking up to suspects like a giant in a children's book, swaying from side to side with each thunderous step. That would be enough to cause a rapscallion to hand himself in whilst confessing to anything. Maybe standing in a puddle of wee-wee too.

I was glad he was on our side and chirped a 'good

morning,' to him, flashing my charming smile. Secretly, I hoped to get a lift from the gruff goliath, but all I got back was a grunt of hello as the beard continued to massively masticate.

'Like, how big was that sandwich originally for him to still be chewing,' I thought, careful to not say that out loud. I wasn't even sure he had mastered English as he stepped into the downpour, probably choosing to converse with ancient runes or some mythic dialect that had to be sung by a quartet of equal voluminous Vikings. The lights of the BMW blinked on and in the rainfall, it looked as close to a hungry chequerboard tiger as anything could physically be.

Both car and giant were eager for the hunt, and as he approached the vehicle I'm sure I saw a nod of salute to it. The rain that hit him seemed to crack and splinter, like glass to concrete, afraid to dampen his clothes.

Balls.

I'm walking then, clearly. Cheers, Sven.

'Stall, find another driver'. I planned. 'A good PC never gets wet', I remembered from training. Nope, wasn't going to be a rule to live by today.

I stepped out and immediately regretted my life choices.

Running into the weather, I hoped to find some solace in a church, shop, or anywhere I could offer some crime prevention advice or local reassurance.

Maybe even grab another coffee?

It was a rule of thumb when out on patrol that you knew where you could get a nice drink and more importantly, oh so much more importantly, where you could go to the loo. There was nothing like getting caught short in the middle of nowhere, in uniform, and then an incident occurred. That was a nightmare that would wake me up with a start.

"A dashingly interesting Police Officer was caught urinating in a park today causing the entire Metropolitan Police Service to be abolished," the headline would read. The media is always so fair on us bobbies.

I was walking, no, sloshing five minutes into duty as the rain continued to hate me. I made sure to wave at a few residents who were coming out of their houses, on their way to normal people's jobs, and they shrugged, waving hellos as they ran into the downpour, hunting for any form of dry transport.

At least they couldn't say the designated ward officers,' most hated line;

"We never see you!" which is like claws on a chalkboard to us. Well spoiler alert; we never see you either. I've always wanted to reply with that, but I'm a nice guy, so I'll just keep it forever in my head.

Thoroughly wet now, I just wanted to get somewhere warm and dry off a tad. Luckily, the waterproof jacket was earning its name, keeping most of the underclothes and equipment from the worst of the water.

I turned the corner and found my crumbling oasis.

The building was massive, with houses upon houses linked together to form the retirement home, the size of which brochures could only dream of. The walls stretched upwards to three floors, all housing people in need of more care than their families could spare the time for. The building fared better than the poorly maintained gardens, though, as they felt the current weather's ravages. Winter was not a careful gardener to this building's exterior foliage, with some plants retreating, to reawaken in the spring.

It could do with a lick of paint here and there too, but I thought that the owners should be splashing any spare cash on some sexy double glazing. That would keep the old codgers a whole lot warmer, and from my viewpoint, securer. The well-lit path to the reception was enticing in the dim of the morning, beckoning this weary police officer inside.

'Like a water slide on a hot day,' I mused. 'Let's slide on into their biscuit barrel!' I secretly hoped for a jaffa cake or three, that I would have to eat otherwise it would be bordering on anti-social behaviour.

I strode up the path and headed towards the comforting reception, safe in the knowledge that nothing bad ever happens in care homes.

Right?

Chapter Seven

Gerald sat staring out of the window most days. He couldn't remember first sitting down. Couldn't even remember where the window led. It was obviously to the outside world, but where though? Was he still near home?

He didn't know that either.

But something seemed different today. He felt lighter than normal, a weight lifted from his shoulders even if just a little.

It was still raining and a man was striding up to reception through the downpour. The dark figure wasn't normally there and was a break from the normal bleak, empty darkness, the rain, and the terrible garden. He looked at the figure but his eyes kept refocusing on his face in the glass of the window. They blurred in and out, and he rubbed them so that he could concentrate on the man beyond but it was too late. His mind was now thinking about his reflection.

He no longer remembered much of himself, but the wrinkled lines crossing his sunken features carved out his life story. The tales they told would forever be lost to him and the fleeting people he'd interacted with through the years as the diagnosed dementia ate away at his memories, ripping the days from his mind. They fell like metaphorical paper calendar dates, disappearing once disconnected from the host.

"Tell him the first story, Gerald." Spoke a female voice from somewhere behind him.

The old man shook his head as much as he'd risk, in

an attempt to clear his mind. He was struggling to find the correct reality layer and he rubbed at his eyes again to help maintain any sort of focus.

He tried to look around the hobby room, in a vain attempt to find the person who uttered the comment, but no one seemed to be in audible range. He went back to looking out the window, concluding that the words were an imaginary figment.

Confusion continued to addle his mind, clouding his vision. He brought a skeletal hand to his face again and wiped his eyes, unsure if the man walking up the pathway was also a phantom of his mind.

'Maybe it was the water running down the double glazing that had created the anomalous image?' he thought as the rain continued to drizzle down the window.

The rain.

'Why was it always raining as well? Every single day,' he moaned aloud. Constant pouring, constant drizzle, constant storms. There was never a flood though which was strange with the sheer amount of water drenching the outside.

The nurses were… Where were they today?

"You're all alone Gerald. It's time to tell him the story, Gerald." The lost voice spoke again and again, no one was there. Just the voice, spitting out the words, venom encasing both syllables of his name.

A nurse passed as he scanned the area but the disjointed voice had not come from her. The voice was older than the young attendants could have been. There was a raspiness to it and whilst female, he thought he heard an undertone hidden behind the vocal sound, echoed voices in different tones.

The nurse continued to attend to her duties, giving Gerald a polite smile on her way past which, while nice, cemented the fact that she was not the one vocalising such a hate-laden sentence.

Looking back out of the window, the man was no longer there.

'Must've been a figment,' he concluded. 'Why was it always raining as well? Every single day.'

Gerald sat staring out of the window most days. He couldn't remember first sitting down. Couldn't even remember where the window led to.

But something seemed different about this day. He suddenly felt the urge to look around again, back into the lobby room. It felt more like a craving, stimulated by some unseen need. He twisted as much as his broken body would allow to satiate the stimulus driving his attention. Standing in the room was a police officer who was talking to the nurse from earlier.

'Why was he here?' Gerald thought, holding back a wave of panic that had filled him for a reason unknown.

"Tell him" came the voice once more.

Chapter Eight

The whirling mass of voices and emotions swirled in the inky darkness. Each entity clamoured for the light which was currently a pinprick in the distance and would need a monumental effort to get even inches closer. There were desperate bids to be the dominant voice as one stepped over another, pushing the weaker among them further back. Some of the forms within, allowed the stronger voices to ring out on their behalf, knowing that they would never have the chance to speak for them all.

But this collective knew what all the imprisoned wanted though. To be free, but more so, to avenge the fallen. 'It's time. Time to tell the story,' they said in unison.

Start with the cause, then move through the pain, the anguish, the fire.

'It isn't very long now. The stories need to be told.' There was an air of anticipation that was growing within. They all knew, they all craved to be heard.

'Someone needs to hear us, or the stories will languish forever as just words without someone to hear them. We know they are jumbled now Gerald, so we will help you.' Again, the anticipation began to move the mass nearer the light. All within moved in synchronicity, an undulating mass of hatred and despair.

'We will help you tell your tales. To tell them before the rain stops. Tell them while you still draw breath. Before we take your last breath, and you join us in the Forever Torment.

You'll never be lonely here in the darkness, here with us. So to the stories, Gerald. Tell them all...'

Chapter Nine

The lobby was an instant relief. It brought the world from grey and wet to an almost sepia warmth that made me want to mould myself into one of the old chairs further into the lobby. I could have easily melted into one of the uncomfortable-looking seats and even at this early hour, the reheating made me want a nap. I could've napped. But not in this soggy getup though. I could see the headlines now;

'Dashingly handsome police officer caught napping on the job.' It would be something like that. Not exactly that, but close and would come with a sneer from the high-ups.

Said lobby was a large open-plan reception room, with various artworks, mainly of nondescript landscapes and wildernesses. A couple of boats filled the water scenes, but not speed boats or anything fun, just big sailboats ambling to nowhere. They were prints in whatever horrible frames the care home's owners could drag out of a skip and didn't match, which set my teeth on edge. One of the sailing boats was straighter on the ocean than the frame on the wall and I gently nudged it level as I passed. I don't think I could've gotten any further on with my day with that wonky picture jarring my mental images.

I missed the sea because it meant that I would be on holiday. However, I much preferred a swimming pool as the sand tended to get caught everywhere in hairy areas, only to be found later when emptying my swimming drawers.

The pool was always my first choice as Mrs Chambers

could relax with one of her gazillion books, taking in the sun, and I could splosh about in the water staring at her marvellous melons. The very thought of her in a bikini added to the growing warmth feeling, this one however resonated outward from a single point. Nope, nope, nope, I'm in an elderly care home. Think of literally anything else and not her perfect pair. Alex! No more fruit metaphors!

I quickly looked back at the pictures on the walls for a distraction and noticed one with a wagon stuck in a river.

'What a silly farmer, you're going to need the AA to tow you out of that one Mr ole McDonald…,' I concluded internally, glad to have avoided the growing crisis.

I was still trying not to think about holidays when a, I'm going to say nurse, greeted her hello. Don't judge me, it was a uniform that didn't match mine, ergo, nurse. She wasn't wearing a firefighter helmet, so again, a nurse. Also, no cats, so not a vet. I should be a bloody detective.

"Hello there officer, is everything alright?" A concerned voice came. It was joined with a look of concern at my very presence.

'Why, oh why, must something always be wrong?' I thought getting a little irked. I mean, there generally is when I get anywhere, but once, just once, I'd like to be greeted without an 'oh shit, insert unknown calamity has happened,' look.

Most people's conversations started with them talking to me like a squirrel in headlights, so reassurance was always my opening reply. It came with the uniform, unfortunately. (I didn't use deer there in my trite metaphorical analogy because, to me, the little fluffy buggers are more frantic).

On this occasion though, the only incident that had happened was that I was considerably damp and maybe dripping.

Moist. *Giggle*.

I smiled back at the woman in both politeness and because I had managed to say the 'M,' word for the second time this morning, albeit in my head.

I ambled over to her with my best 'it's all ok,' manner with hands open and empty, body language one oh one. Top tip if a police officer has a pocket notebook in their hands, poo has most definitely hit the wind propulsion device.

Greeting the young woman, I checked her name pin enough to read it, but not enough to be boob-shamed. 'Melody,' was proclaimed there, read quickly by my eagle eye from the emblazoned on the blue and white plastic boob badge.

"You don't have to be mad to work here..." I said, putting the name badge and the dad jokes meme together. I regretted that one as it was, and always had been a terrible joke. Even though deftly put, it was greeted with a definite 'huh?' look, so I immediately knew my humour was going to fall on deaf ears or possibly an empty mind. Jokes are almost always less humorous when you have to explain them afterwards...

"I'm Alex" I continued, bringing the young nurse's brain back into gear. I would normally, out of habit, add in the rank number but didn't want to overburden her with a maths equation at this point. Start slow.

"Welcome to Shady Oaks care home. I'm Melody." I

was going to respond with my razor-sharp Sherlockian detective skills that I already knew her name, but that might confuse her further. I even held back the 'no shit, Watson,' because in the past, even an 'I know,' had brought forth a torrent of letters which when strung together, I'm told, was a version of English.

"Oi Bruv. How'd you know wot I done? I ain't done nuffink fed! You can't touch me pig, I pay your wages!" When they had indeed done summink and hadn't paid anyone anything. Oh, the irony.

"I was hoping to get a bit warmer and wait for the rain to ease up. I'm a tad moist!" I hoped the wetness statement would be more her humour level. (Also moist x3). Again, an audible whoosh as that zinger went flying out the window too. My wit is lost on these mere mortals...

Mel was in her mid-twenties, about 5,' 3," white, and of average build. Even my descriptions are written in police language but you get the drift. She was wearing a uniform adorned with the Shady Oaks logo which, in a stroke of marketing genius, was an oak tree.

'That will be one thousand pounds please', I imagined the marketing department saying, proud of their bespokely innovative tree.

She was pleasant enough, even though she did not appreciate the gags so far. Her practised smile wasn't one of those gritted-teeth ones and carried the care her role needed, so she wasn't dead inside just yet and still carried enough warmth to say that she did indeed give more than two shits. I had hoped that the charm would work its magic and get me another tea spot* for the books.

*Tea spots are a term used by officers for safe places to grab a cuppa and more importantly a quick wee when out and about. Some research was needed first though as to the cleanliness of said facilities, the size of the coffee mugs and the quality of the biscuit-based treats.

I surveyed the room past her as she smiled and showed me inside.

"Would you like to chat with some of our residents? You could give them some advice about crime!" She chirped.

No shit, Sher... Nope, held that one back too. I try to only ever swear in my head as letting one slip in uniform is like farting at a funeral.

"Doing or preventing?" I responded. Again tumbleweeds. I do give up now.

The hobby room was extensive, hidden from an exterior eye by large plants and a flat-screen TV. The screen was tuned to old people's programs about gardening or archaeology or some such as was their choice at this early hour. A presenter whose career had died with the advent of more than three channels was trying to look interested as a gentleman pointed to a hedge. Said professor of foliage was clearly out of his depth being filmed and spluttered over his specialist subject.

Yes, I could definitely nap here.

Well-thumbed books littered the various side tables dotted around the room, taken from a wooden shelving unit in the corner. I noted a fair few spy thrillers from the distinguished authors of yesteryear, with the classic Tinker adorning the spines of both hard and soft cover versions. The Mills and Boons were also there, which I felt was a bit harsh in this environment.

'Here's what you used to get up to, you old fogey,' was basically what they were saying. The bullseye equivalent of 'here's what you could've won,' from the old darts program. Mental note, update references when talking about elderly vaginas.

An obligatory chess set sat proudly on top of Ludo, Draughts, Snakes and Ladders, and a larger one, containing all the classics in one single box. I chuckled as the collected compendium had the exact same games in it that sat upon it. This giggle would've been lost on young Melody but small things for hilarious minds as the saying goes.

But she was showing me around, so playing nice was the game at hand. Win trust and earn coffee.

There were four people in the room, all easily in their eighties or above. Two were looking at the screen as the man was still pointing at bushes and I actually thought one of the people watching the telly had unfortunately passed until he coughed up a lung. Another was deep in a book, not of a tinkered variety.

The last one was a solitary man, sitting staring out of the window. I could only see him from behind initially but imagined him swinging the chair around with a cat on his lap, à la a James Bond villain.

Headcount taken, I scanned the room looking for the important thing, the coffee station but got a definite feeling that I was being watched. Had Oldfinger turned menacingly in the chair to look my way? Was he going to outline his entire world domination plan before letting me escape to heroically thwart his minions?

'Please be holding a cat. Stroke it like your devious plan is almost complete! Then throw in a 'Mwahahahaha,' for good measure,' I hoped, my mental fingers crossed.

He was in his eighties, at a guess, and was frail and hunched over, even sitting in the high-backed chair. The grey wisps of hair on the back of his head reached down to his collar, retreating from where it once lived atop his head. He looked like he was propped up by the chair alone, which must've helped his staring out into nothingness life goal. Maybe he was waiting for a family member to pop around with a tin of biscuits adorned with a scene from old times? Their overly buttery contents were not going anywhere near my tea, I thought, even though I had neither beverage nor biscuit.

"That's Gerald" Melody lyrically informed me even though I hadn't asked. "He's been here for years. No visitors and never said a word. Seems in there behind his eyes though, but must be lost elsewhere in the thought process. The poor old soul."

Surprisingly thoughtful and poignant from Melody, but whilst showing her caring nature, she was missing the torment I was going through, as this avenue of conversation brought me no closer to a boiled beverage.

'Selfish fictitious family members,' I grumbled, 'not showing up and bringing their friendly neighbourhood police officer a treat. How rude'.

I actually felt sorry for the old dude though, I mean, what sort of life did he have just sitting there? At least push him in front of the telly so he could follow whatever crap BBCpoo was showing.

"The visiting GP says he has dementia and is not long for this world" she whispered, as if she was going to be heard by the spying octogenarians. Turning to the nurse, I offered a slight deal.

"Well if I could grab a tea, maybe I could just sit with him for a bit. Might make him feel a bit comfortable and reassured?" She nodded and trotted off to a trolley in the corner and prepared what is clearly going to be a lukewarm cup of piss. Please to god, furnish me with a garibaldi or chocolate hobnob.

I turned back and Gerald was still staring at me. No cat to be seen.

Chapter Ten

I looked at the old man who was now transfixed with me and thought it a wee bit creepy. He must've heard us chatting somehow and wondered who was disturbing his routine of staring into the empty abyss. Those massive 'old man ears,' radar detecting his name most probably.

Or he just realised no biscuits were incoming as his fictional family had fucking forgotten. Bastards. I needed a chocolate hobnob now to get over the abandonment of the fake family I just made up.

I've made eye contact now, so I'm committed to at least a 'hello,' I thought. I smiled at the old codger who was following my approach with the same blank, gaunt expression, his eyes the only thing that confirmed life was still present. His face seemed to convey a multitude of emotions, but sadness seemed to be the overall outward winner. Or should that actually be the loser? I felt sorry for the old gent who had obviously seen a thing or two in his time, his memories lost behind the wall of his diagnosed dementia.

At least he wouldn't miss my jokes. Just every word I uttered, the poor sod.

I risked a subtle wave matched with a polite smile. I hoped that this would be enough pleasantries and I could get on with the increasingly important task of beverage consumption. But no, he still wanted to stare at me, so I resigned myself to going and having a chat, albeit one-sided.

'Come on Mel, get the kettle on! I might be male, but even I can multitask!' I thought frustratedly as she tended to one of her patrons.

I walked over to Gerald in my politely open manner, as I did not want a heart attack on my conscience. My Emergency Life Support training was up to date, but I thought if I was doing chest compressions and 'another one bites the dust,' came to mind, there would be chaos. It's got the right tempo, but the wrong words on every level.

Walking back past the crappy paintings and further away from my cup of tea, I noticed that the old duffer was sitting near a radiator, so a small win there.

As I got to his side, I dragged across a similar armchair to Gerald's. It was threadbare on one armrest, the pattern disappearing into the now exposed lining. I began removing some of my layers too, hanging my jacket over a radiator to my right, hoping it was on to warm the rain off. Now, I try to leave the Metvest on at all times whilst out-out, but I was hidden away in an old folk's home so took the negligible risk. What's the worst that could happen right? The worst that could happen was a chance encounter with a slip and then a hot beverage spillage disaster, but that occurrence was getting ever further away it felt. A Metvest wasn't stopping that either, so...

Placing the heavy protective vest to the side of the chair, I stood it up to help keep its form. You have to hang these things up normally to keep the plates inside in the right place, so standing it upright was currently the best available option. I had been through numerous coat pegs as the weight of the thing buckled and broke the less hardy of hangers.

I sat down, creaking the chair below me. The arse accommodation was not used for someone who weighed more than the normal resident bone bags, and the seat continued to groan grumpily under my weight. Almost enough to give me a bit of a complex actually. It was comfy enough though and it held my weight thankfully, albeit under protest, and I now returned Gerald's gaze.

This man was skeletal. His hands were thin to the point I could see veins. The yellow of his nails told me that he is, or at least has been a smoker, the index and middle fingernails cracked beyond any manicurist's skillset. A slight scar on his wrist disappeared up his arm and under the warm-looking dressing gown. I thought it looked a bit like an industrial accident such was the length of the healed cut. Or maybe it was an old war wound or some such?

Under his gown was a classic pair of blue and white striped pyjamas that everyone's grandad owned, even down to the standard moccasin fluffy slippers. You must get given the 'old person kit,' upon hitting sixty, alongside the 'louder than hell,' button for the telly, I mused hilariously.

'That's one to ask Gerald when our glittering conversation dies,' I thought.

His gaunt face looked as though it was falling floorward, not helped by his slightly open mouth. Teeth were haphazardly placed inside his mouth having lost a few alongside his memories of how. The point of his chin only added to the look that he was melting into the earth, which I really hoped wasn't today. It would be a tonne of paperwork, the headlines, but mainly, I never wish death upon anyone, even the worst of the bad guys.

I snapped back into my description of the old man as

the eyes of Gerald told a very different story altogether. They were steely grey, any colour long having left the building and at this point, the only real sign anyone was driving the Gerald mobile. The lights were on as the pupils followed my movement, the driver behind keeping a watchful eye on my presence. They had a life to them though and I thought that this was indeed where the 'Gerald,' was.

I'd seen these eyes before though, but couldn't place where. I shrugged it off as a daydream glitch, as I have a habit of narrating my life in my head. You may have noticed this.

He continued to stare at me as I looked for my cup of warming tea water to arrive, hoping upon hope that she would have at least one sugar.

Gerald however continued to stare intently, as his mouth began to creak open.

Chapter Eleven

Gerald sat staring out of the window most days. He couldn't remember first sitting down. Couldn't even remember where the window led to. It was obviously to the outside, but where though? He didn't know that either. It was outside. And this morning there was a man there. But he had disappeared now, leaving the view outside as drab and grey as it always is.

Just leaving the rain.

'Why was it always raining as well? Every single day,' he moaned. 'Constant pouring, constant drizzle, constant storms'. There was never a flood though which was strange with the sheer amount of water drenching the outside.

Gerald was looking through the window into the eternal wet abyss beyond when he thought he heard something from behind him. It wasn't the disjointed voice from earlier. That had just been his thoughts and memories playing tricks on him, he'd concluded.

It seemed to be happening more and more these days as the old man drew further and further into the pit of his dementia prison. His thoughts seemed more inaccessible each day as they disappeared into an inky blackness within his mind. It crept up, enclosing rational thought and relieving him of past deeds. It clawed through his memories, chewing them, and spitting them into the depths, no longer needed. Names, places, and details had all left him, and people's faces had followed, lost to his mind.

Gerald also felt a weight on his shoulders today, pressing down on his weak frail frame, threatening to squash and crunch him further into the chair. He felt urged to do something, an achievement different from the standard lonely existence he normally expected.

More voices.

Not the one from earlier, thankfully. He reminded himself that the female voice from earlier was an illusion caused by his own sickness. A misfiring synapse as it gave its last breath.

A stirring filled him, he felt as if he was losing control of his faculties. It was an unnerving feeling that brought thoughts of his end. Is this what happens? Is this how a person dies? No, he thought. This was worse. He felt no internal changes, like his heart slowing or skipping, this was as if he was being puppeted. Controlled on strings, and pulled into a position he was not able to fight against. His head was turning to his left and he was immediately confused by the action as he wasn't able to stop it. There was no control, an involuntary movement of his weak and frail form. His gaze was being moved from his window into the hobby room which he cared not for.

He gripped the armrests with what little strength he had left in his body, but his dwindling strength failed him.

It wasn't enough. He continued turning.

He wanted to call a care worker, the nice one that sang, but his words had been lost to him for a time now. Like love letters washed away in the sand. He'd almost forgotten the sound of his own voice.

It was at this moment he felt the movement. He was off to his left and approached differently to the nurses as they spoke immediately upon getting near his chair.

This was to not startle the guests, he thought.

He kept trying to fight against the movement as he could not order his body back under his control, and he finally turned to see the man in the hobby room.

It was a police officer.

He could help.

He'll stop the turning. He'll help me stay in this chair as a fall would definitely break something unfixable.

Gerald was panicking inside his head as he worried about the incoming fall which would crack his head on the floor, or at best break a frail arm. He expected, planned even, to die in his sleep, not the crunching agony of a fall he could not defend against.

'Please…,' The word formed in his head but was blocked, held there motionless, unable to blossom into anything resembling a cry for help. He was helpless and he hated this feeling.

He wanted control back. He wanted to be the one making the decisions again. He needed the power once more offered to all living things.

Gerald noticed the lawman wave and smile welcomingly, clearly oblivious to the old man's predicament. Was he ever going to come and help? Unable to talk, the octogenarian tried to change his facial expression into one of plight.

The police officer started coming over.

He was coming to stop me! Gerald risked a glimmer of hope which was brightened by the fact that the turning had stopped. He was left staring at the oncoming man, still stuck, like a waxwork in an old remote museum.

The officer sat down after removing his coat and protective vest and Gerald realised that his head was following the officer's movements. He knew fighting back against the action was fruitless, so resigned himself to the good news that he was still upright.

The policeman was kind of face under a bristled, greying beard. Standing at what Gerald could guess as about five foot nine, he thought the man was erring on the side of heavy, but proportioned well for a man his age.

The black of the uniform was different from when he was a boy. He was sure there was more of a navy blue hue to it back then. The equipment had also changed too. The whistle had been replaced with a small black recording device, the truncheon now an extendable asp.

His train of thought was broken with the proclamation of; "Hi, I'm PC Alex Chambers. I hear you're Gerald." It was said in a way that didn't expect an answer with a face smiling, and filled with care. As he spoke, he occasionally looked past the elderly man's chair as if awaiting the arrival of the first course of a promised meal, but his attention was Gerald's for the most part.

The elderly man felt something happening in his throat. Was it thirst? He couldn't remember or discern the feeling. His mouth dried out long ago.

His jaw began to move.

"I have stories," rasped Gerald. The sound of his voice shocked him as it had been years since he'd been able to utter even the briefest of requests.

The crash of the tea cup concluded his sentence and remained broken as the story began.

Numb

A Short Story By Gerald Heggarty

1

Late October 1951.

Wars had been fought and won. All signs of death and destruction had been cleared away from the streets of London in an attempt to keep a cautious hope alive. Prime Minister Winston Churchill, the hero of the devastating World War, won his re-election, returning him to power after a brief time away.

Things were settling, changing to a new, possibly even optimistic normal. Tentative steps were taken to regular life. One where you could go about your normal business, not stopping to think about running and hiding from vicious shelling, bombarding streets at random. Houses were being rebuilt, and with them, dreams. The destruction of the Second World War was painted over, but never truly forgotten, a wound forever felt deep within.

But the bustling London life seemed like a hundred miles away from the small basement flat in Wandsworth.

The borough was formed from five civil parishes: Clapham, Putney, Streatham, Tooting Graveney, and Wandsworth. In 1904, these five were combined into a single civil parish called Wandsworth Borough, which was conterminous with the metropolitan borough. The suburb housed many families striving for more. All of them wanted to move on from the wars and devastation of years gone by, all needing and yearning for new, safer times.

Within this borough was Clapham Common Northside, which was home to the Gardener family. Before living here, the patriarch's parents had resided there, leaving the home to their only child and the outside world; this husband, wife, and two children were the definition of idyllic. A standard among families of the time.

There were smiles in the park.

Hands were held whilst out walking.

Happy and playful.

It became anything but, one dark, and stormy night.

*

John Gardener was a strapping, muscular man, born from good stock and solid parenting. Not one to be spared the birch as a child, John had grown into a tough hard-working man who supported Jane, his wife of eleven years. His black hair was lustrous even though the beginnings of grey started showing through underneath the full mane. The hair continued down into distinctive, well-trimmed sideburns, common of the time.

At thirty-one, the pair had married in their twenties in a hopeful time, though put to the test in later years. Through terrible times, both lost relatives to the war, both then craving the security of the other. This bond had sired two offspring, Tom, a boy of ten, and Nancy, six.

Tom was a normal boy into normal things. He had aspirations of one day following in his father's footsteps and learning the tools of his patriarch's trade, whilst Nancy was busy learning all she could at school. An avid reader, she seemed to inhale any book that she could find, all topics and genres, both fiction and non. John didn't see the point in her education though as she was obviously going to be marrying into the life of the typical housewife, much like his wife.

If only he knew.

Both children attended a good local school, and all expenses were paid for by their parent's employment. John worked long hours in metal manufacturing while his wife had started a clerical role, much to John's anger. But they needed money, so he had relented and allowed her to work for a local typing agency. This was authorised under the proviso that when no longer needed, she would leave the company, and also the hours she worked had to suit her duties as mother. 'Children don't raise themselves', he thought. So she was told that all the children's needs were met at the detriment of her job, not his, as hers was a secondary consideration.

As it should be.

'And rightly so,' thought John, allowing the current norms of the day to back up his choices for his wife.

The employment situation complicated their relationship as John was quick to rile, to the smallest of things.

'It would be better if Jane stayed home. She should be caring for the kids and preparing the house for us all.' John began to feel the pressure building behind his eyes and his temper flared. These thoughts rose within him on an almost daily basis, causing him to have to take stock of his temperament.

Even the smallest things would cause him to either withdraw into himself and a whiskey glass or storm out to the nearest pub. He would return only when he could be sure his wife and children were asleep, to not start the argument once again. He knew his anger would lead to an eruption of furious violence, so kept himself in check.

His tactic was avoidance of issues, keeping his counter arguments to himself was working as the worst the couple had faced was arguments. Even though he felt correct, he did not want to drive Jane and the children away as he was acutely aware of his temper. He promised himself that he would not be the hard taskmaster his father was, but the years of parental conditioning made this all but impossible.

Each morning, any altercation was all but swept away, forgotten, and undealt with. It was bottled up, labelled and shelved within John, but each new unaided scar festered in their relationship.

Jane's independence from him was an almost weekly catalyst in the latter weeks of 1951, but it was in the spring of 1952 that he first struck Jane.

Alcohol was the stimulant.

Money was proclaimed as the reason.

A backhand swipe was the darkness within him overflowing into the real world. This was the night that would bring change to so many lives going forward.

Tom looked across the table as his father's hand swiped outward, swooshing through the air to connect with Jane's face. The fist was still partially clenched when it was placed back on the table, opposite from his other in a stance like he was still awaiting dinner.

It was unexpected.

Out of nowhere.

An occurrence never to have even been hinted at previously.

He saw his mother burst into tears as her lip began making its injury clear. Blood began seeping from the wound on the left side of Jane's mouth, a look of shock completing her astonishment. She immediately burst into tears and left the room, scooping up Nancy in her arms. She motioned her head for Tom to follow, but both children could not fully comprehend what had happened at the dinner table that night. Nancy, a mess of tears was carried away, leaving Tom frozen in place. Jane managed to grab a napkin on her way out, holding it to her face while her other arm carried the crying little girl.

Shock gave way to anger, which was venomously clear in her eyes.

As she swept away the fury was apparent, even to the young boy, a loathing he had not seen from his mother before. Her eyes were piercing through her assailant as she moved, striking him like fire.

The small boy heard his sister whimpering, as she disappeared into the bedroom, still carried in her mother's arms. Jane slammed the door, but it creaked open ajar having not caught on the latch correctly, due to the angry thrust of force from the wounded parent. Each noise was made evermore audible due to the silence at the dinner table, which seemed to last an eternity as the two generational males sat there immobile. Tom guessed, and hoped, that thoughts were flashing through his father's mind to try and make sense of the situation, to find a fix. He hoped that the older man was working out how to apologise and sort this terrible nightmare out.

There seemed no cause to the ten-year-old boy, no rhyme or reason for the vicious outburst. There had never been violence at home.

Nothing, ever. Yes, there had been arguments, but never violent bloodshed. The most brutality he had seen was some minor bullying from the older kids in his school, stealing the younger ones,' dinner money, but this generally just resulted in a clip round the ear from the sternest male teacher.

None of the bullies tried anything on with Tom for some reason though, which he was thankful for. Lucky, he guessed.

Still, they sat, for what felt like painfully long moments.

Tom watched the food his mother had prepared with love almost whither as it began to grow cold in front of him. With a quiet movement, he reached forward to try and reach one of the juicy chicken drumsticks that were attached to the large cooked bird in the centre of the table. The whole chicken was a Wednesday treat and they would feast on it, with all the trimmings, plus have enough for tasty sandwiches the following day. It was a beloved tradition in the Gardener's residence, one his father was proud of. It showed cautious opulence and that everything was working out, a symbol for all to see and reassurance for John that he was indeed doing his fatherly duty well.

Tom's eyes moved from the perfectly cooked food to his father who had remained stationary since the incident. His eyes darted between food and father, unsure what to do. He was unaware of how long had passed since the outburst, the shock of the punch seemingly causing issues with time's natural flow.

The smell alone drove him forward. Wafting towards him, tempting him to taste. The hunger that enticed him was born of a desperate need for normalcy but also pure greed. The food would solve all his problems and make everything better and as he had had a full day of physical education, and then the rugby that followed, he was all but famished.

Starved, he found himself rubbing his belly in anticipation of the succulent food he was about to enjoy. Everything would go back to normal if they all had dinner and his father apologised.

He would eat. His mother and sister would be at the table and nothing would've happened, the incident wiped from the family's lives. Yes, he needed to eat, to reset them all.

His enrapture meant that he did not see the knife.

2

The young child, a mere ten years old, had only seen blood from cuts and grazes made from rambunctious youthful endeavours. A climbed tree brought a scrape to the elbow due to an unseen branch, or a tumble whilst playing in the tarmacked school playground.

His bicycle had left him with a nasty knee graze when trying to navigate a particularly rocky downhill in the local park, but that was the worst injury he'd seen on a human being.

Even the blood from the strike to his mother was minimal as she had put a hand to her face quickly as instinct and shock took over. She had snatched up a table napkin from in front of her, both to mop the wound and more importantly hide the injury from the children's memories.

Tom's peripheral vision caught the flash of a knife blade from the corner of his eye as his father struck out once again. This time though, the larger male had picked up a knife, possibly ready for the incoming food as Tom was.

The boy had reached forward with his left hand to grab an enticing chicken leg while his father was holding a knife with his right. The movement in front of the emotional parent had awoken him and he had slashed forward, arcing the blade in hand.

The tip had caught Tom just at the wrist, lashing upwards towards his elbow for ten inches until his father's assaulting arc brought the blade away. Luckily for the small boy, the damage was on the top of his arm so missed the arteries hidden below.

John hadn't made a sound the entire attack. His hand with the blooded knife came back to rest next to his empty plate, his face still emotionless. The entire movement was a silent, fluid motion that shocked the young boy into his seat, his body clenching in shock and fear.   —

As the knife glinted in the grip of his father, a drop of blood dripped from the top down onto the hilt and then to the white-knuckled hand holding it. Tom's fear at his father's sudden movement caused him to raise both arms in front of his face in self-defence, not realising at this point that his arm was pouring blood down to his elbow. It began pooling on the table and he began to whimper audibly as the shock and pain, alongside the preceding incident built his emotions into a desperate outpouring of panicked fear.

From behind his defensive posture, Tom felt the viscous liquid splash on his leg. A steady drip drip drip made him look down to see the dark red of the blood now beginning to cover his school trousers.

Then the pain hit him even harder than before due to the realisation of the exact damage to his arm. It screeched up his arm like fire to petrol, sending a scream of agony to his brain. As Tom turned his arm, and the hand to see the injury in more detail, the muscle and skin stretched causing the lacerated arm to send more blood throbbing from the wound. Whilst not bone-deep, it was long enough to be bleeding profusely.

The greatest wound the boy had currently ever seen. This would be a core memory to stay with him for years to come.

Tom opened his mouth to scream but no sound came out. He rose from his chair agape, looking at the man he once considered a role model, an icon, a parent. Stumbling as the pain clouded his judgement and tears welled up in his eyes, he fell backwards, landing awkwardly on his bottom, unable to stop himself due to the ravaged arm and his other hand clutching around the injury, trying to hold it closed.

His young mind grasped for anything to help reason the situation into normalcy, but it had settled on stopping blood escape. Logic would have to wait until first aid was administered.

He stared up at his father who had risen from his seat.

A warm feeling began spreading from his trousers as the thought of further wounds made him urinate uncontrollably. Tears flooded down his cheeks and the boy was lost to panic, as the acrid smell of urine mixed with the coppery tones of the blood.

Still, without a word, the towering man got up and moved towards the bedroom.

3

The sound of John's footsteps echoed around the room as he moved away from his injured son. The sound of his crying reached the man but did not trigger any of the correct parental responses. The urge to rush to his son's aid, to defend him whilst administering the caring first aid was lost to the detached father.

Nor did it prompt any emotion whatsoever. The crying was distant and muffled by the thoughts going through the man's head. They were a jumbled mess to his senses as if he was screaming unintelligibly into his deaf ears.

His mind had broken.

He was no longer controlling his actions.

His emotional state had collapsed into the husk of what was his rational thought process. Everything felt numb, even the sounds around him began to be anaesthetised in his senses.

Now, he was being driven purely by anger, a rage at the spectres in his home. These doppelgängers had replaced the warmth of his family with a cold detached void.

He needed to hurt them, to rid the world of these demons.

John's macrocosmic existence had snapped earlier that day when, having finished work early, went to surprise Jane with a surprise apology lunch. The realisation had dawned on him that he was being unreasonable with, not just her work, but Jane's independence.

This beautiful dove that he married was everything to him. She was a goddess who needed to be free so that she would return each day to his loving embrace. Such an encircle of warmth had not been there in as long as he could remember, their arguments driving a wedge where love lived.

Today was a day of change though.

Today they would begin again. He would try to shelve his antiquated ideals, making them a thing of the past, not their future. Love would be renewed and rekindled, flamed by this first gesture.

He would cherish this angel in their home who had brought the loves of his life, Tom and Nancy into this world. This family needed a protector, and he was it, the defending knight of their realm.

He'd been a fool to treat her this way.

But he'd been a fool to trust her.

Looking up at the office building she worked in, he watched as a blind was lowered in the window of a small office. Before the slats had hidden his view, he saw his beloved, naked from the waist up. She was looking at a nondescript person with eagerness in her eyes, with a longing gaze he had all but forgotten.

She leaned back against a desk and jumped up to sit there, her pert breasts visible even from her husband's obscured viewpoint. But it was her smile that caught him, not her nakedness in the presence of another. The look on her face was the one that had entrapped him in the first place. Mischievous, playful, and loving.

But her vision was now for another. A person he could not see clearly as he was transfixed on his beloved wife. He wanted to know who she was looking at but knew it would cause fresh waves of pain because it would never be him again. He savoured this vision whilst it ripped him apart with a crushing anguish.

His feet unconsciously brought him to the window to try and find reason in the madness before him.

Who had tempted Jane away?

He would find this man who had bested him. He wanted to know what this new suitor brought that he never did as rage bubbled within him. It was mixed with a feeling of total desolation and the two crippling emotions battled violently for supremacy.

As best he could, he peered through the blind obscuring the view.

He saw the person now kissing Jane frantically, both of them eagerly grabbing at each other. The frantic movement of each other's caress had the same intent as someone grasping for their last meal.

He watched as the pair were entwined, hands everywhere, excited at the feel of each touch which seemed to bring an electric wave of pleasure with each motion. A hand rose up Jane's side and ended at her breast, delicately dancing around the perfect mound.

It seemed to draw each curve expertly and feel every smooth surface with the purest of longing.

He saw Jane's hand move up the other person's back, and her head went back with an ecstatic sigh of pleasure. She clawed at the material of the other person's shirt, pulling it closer in a loving grip.

Jane's hand then continued up and into the woman's long auburn hair.

4

The footsteps grew louder, an ominous thud from the hallway, getting closer as they drew nearer the door. The sound brought a portentous feeling in the pit of stomachs as the spectre of their family member approached.

From where the pair sat, they could see little, the door mostly obscuring the view. It had been slammed with such anger that it had not caught correctly on the old catch and now stood slightly ajar, after coming to rest a foot or so from the frame.

Moments before, they had heard a clatter from the dining room, unaware of the cause. A crash followed, and then the scrape of chair legs grating across the floor as it was moved away from the table.

Fear grew in the woman as she knew that her husband was moving, her son still there with him. She almost got to her feet to help the boy, but a mixture of fear and protection for her daughter held her still. She knew her limits but was caught in the most direst of juxtapositions.

Jane swaddled the small child who was sobbing

uncontrollably in her mother's embrace, cradled but unsure yet of the level of safety, still petrified from the evening's events. She shuddered in the parental embrace and to the small child, the hug was the definition of safety, as it created a warm glow of protection around her.

Everything was going to be alright. It must be.

The room they were in was Jane and John's bedroom, where they had sired both children. It was painted a warm magnolia, with little decoration.

A solitary decorative lamp adorned the corner of the room which stood six feet tall. The bright orange shade seemed to suck the light from the bedroom so was not fit for its purpose. Jane hated this thing too, but it was the last thing John had been given before losing both parents in the war. So they couldn't ever get rid of Death's last gift.

The only other adornment was the copy of the Hay Wain by Constable. It had been there when the couple had moved in and they hadn't found anything to replace it as yet. While the original was considered a masterpiece, painted in 1821, it was not to her liking, and she wanted something more fitting to the modern era.

Something bright and colourful.

Something alive.

Something like Marilynn.

The oak dresser at least was to Jane's taste as it matched the wardrobe that held both their meagre clothing. It had strong oaken drawers that could hold many a folded shirt, its top adorned with a few small framed pictures of happier times that she wished could return.

One such picture displayed their trip to Bournemouth beach where Tom had given his ice cream to a much smaller Nancy after hers had become food for the sand below her feet. The plop of the sweet treat, as it fell from the cone, would stay with her as, when the beginnings of an emotional cry started to cross her face, Tom gallantly leapt forward to save the moment. Both the kids loved the beach there, clamouring to stay as long as possible. It was happier times, a distant memory of the fish and chips on the beach, feeding the seagulls as they swooped and dived. One day, they would live there, John had often promised.

Looking around, Jane knew though that this room was no longer the marital bedroom. This was now her room, one in which John would never set foot in again if she had her way. The love between the couple was all but extinguished from her side now.

This room would usher in a change.

All she wanted to do now though was to see, to feel, Marilynn again. They were each other's destiny, their future hidden until a day when people would accept others for decisions different from their judgments. A day when two people's love was no one else's conversation.

The kids would understand eventually. Hopefully. But if they didn't, the two women would keep it to themselves, even from the children.

Marilynn and Jane had met at work in the typing pool, a room filled with the clickety-clack of both typewriters and heels, the stench of hairspray ever-present. It was a female-only environment for work purposes, only interrupted by some of the more lecherous management figures who would sit on their employees,' desks, expecting the world due to their standing in the business. They'd gaze down on their colleagues, leaving them all feeling polluted, by the typical fat cat's lurid gaze with its clear, slobbering intent.

Jane had never intended anything to happen. She'd always hidden her feelings for women, even to the point of marrying John.

But Marilynn...

She was fire in a dress, a wild spirit clothed in secrecy. She didn't walk through a room, she swooshed, on a glide, her very movements an enticement. She brought a fragrant breeze with her that wafted through the room with a soft delicate scent.

Many men had tried. Many men had failed.

Her auburn hair is what caught Jane's eye. It flowed like a river of autumn leaves and danced behind her, sashaying even without wind to capture it. The fire of the colour matched the very movement with every step.

After seeing that, Jane was lost. All pretences were gone. Boundaries needed to be broken.

Their first touch was as electric as she imagined sending a warmth spiralling through her. Both women's eyes locked at the feeling, both knowing, without words, that they needed to feel each other. In desperate silence, hidden from the world, the pair found their moments.

A brush of a hand when walking past or a hand on each other's back when looking over each other's desk was a tease that brought urgency. And that morning, they had given in to desire and found a little unused office to explore each other in privacy.

The room held various files and a large desk but had been unused for many a year. It was perfect and brought the bliss both knew was coming. A perfect location for their secret tryst.

Jane realised that this was who she had always wanted to be. The freedom was as exhilarating as the other woman's delicate touch. She cried out, quickly muffling her joy with a hand. She remembered the touch, how it first felt under her clothing and longed to be back at their secluded union.

5

The bedroom door opened slowly, the movement bringing her thoughts crashing back to her current facade. This reality was darker than the golden light Marilynn had brought to her heart, and it gave her the strength to begin the fight back to her new love.

Confrontation was needed to crush this man, to show him that he was no longer the man of the house. One was no longer needed in her new world. Her courage would give her this sought-after new normalcy, and bring security to her children's world.

"Why..." The single word uttered was almost a whisper but carried enough weight to be a threat.

John was standing with the main light of the hallway behind him, almost in silhouette. The horrible lamp was on in the corner but the shade continued to imprison light instead of granting it freedom.

"Why what, John? Why did you hit me is more of a

question. Don't you think so?" Anger and adrenaline clouded her words as her mouth pulsed out more pain. She had found strength now, brought on by pain, anger and a motherly protection of her children with the condition of one still unknown.

"Why..." he said again. It was slightly louder this time and had a tone of anger underlying it.

Jane moved her daughter behind her and stood at the end of the bed, her fury at his actions now bringing strength to her words.

"In front of the children, John!" She spoke his name with the venom of an abused woman. She spat it out like poison, a wasp sting removed.

She took a step towards him.

"I know we haven't been getting along for a time now, John, but that was too much. Pack your things!" Each mention of his name was the metaphoric verbal punch in the face the man deserved, her strength bringing new vigour to her fight. It coursed through her now, taking her defiant steps closer to her ex-husband.

She was within striking distance and considered hitting him back, but knew Nancy was behind her watching through her tears. She knew her punch would be ceremonious at best and could bring more violent repercussions. Plus, she wanted to show strength through words, not actions.

"Why her..."

The shock at hearing the words hit Jane in the stomach as hard as the knife which impaled her.

Initially, Jane thought John had hit her again, but it was

a weird strike as his hand was still at the impact point. She stared down at his fist and noticed what looked like a handle in his grip, protruding from near his little finger. At the other end of his hand, blood started to appear as it oozed from above his thumb, clinging to everything it touched. The wooden handle with its gold leaf was quickly dyed red as blood poured forth.

The impact site started to feel warm and she had initially thought that she had wet herself due to the impact. Everything seemed suddenly in question, and she could not fathom how it had come to this. Nothing made sense, what has happened? Her mind danced, unable to comprehend her current crisis.

She stepped back.

As she did, the knife slid outward from the pit of her stomach, the pain screeched into her and up her spine as the blade cut her further on its exit. She bent double, as if to protect the wounded area, stumbling back a step. Looking up, John had not moved, leading her to the conclusion that her withdrawal had led to the knife's extraction.

She opened her mouth to scream as she looked back at the man in front of her, who was now purely a shadow of both the man she knew and the man he had become. But it was cut short as the air in her lungs burst from her as the knife was readied and driven into her a second time. Easily, slicing into her just below the left rib, she gurgled as blood started to fill her lung, the punctured organ collapsing.

She gasped for breath from a respiratory system that was failing her. Her right lung struggled to keep up with the shock and panic that was now taking over Jane. Each breath brought a new wave of agony as it rasped within her.

Again the knife was ripped from her, this time by John and with a brutal fury. It sent blood and matter flying about the room, spattering the sparse decorations. The items within had become dotted with red spots, the once happy photos now ruined and showing the families,' true picture.

Jane's fight-or-flight instinct was all she had left as she fought the urge to both run and protect the now screaming Nancy. She tried to speak, but the effort brought blood into her mouth and she gagged at the taste, spitting it on the floor in front of her. Coughing, she looked at her daughter who sat bolt upright in fear, her face speckled with the expelled crimson fluid.

She turned to look back at the child as the third strike hit her just below the jaw. She felt the blade slice against the third and fourth vertebrae in her neck as blood continued to fill her throat. Breathing was an almost impossible task now, her only working lung filling with blood.

She clawed at both John's hand and the wound, her mind now scrabbling for any hope. Panic took any away though as she concluded that she was going to die, leaving her children in the care of this demon. Tears at the thought of her child's fate poured from her, mixing and diluting the blood covering her face.

She tried to apologise to Nancy, but her blood-filled throat offered up only an unintelligible gurgle.

Her strength then suddenly left her as the knife was torn from her for the last time. As it left its fatal wound, blood arced from the artery, spraying the lamp Jane hated. The fountain covered the set of drawers too, dripping from every handle and outcrop.

As she hit the floor, the blood splattered Hay Wain was the last thing she saw.

The last thing she felt was her hand crushed underfoot as John mashed down on it, a mere annoyance in his way as he stepped closer to his daughter.

6

Tom heard the fight, heard the screams, heard the crying. It was clear that this night would bring more new terrors.

Still sitting on the floor, he hadn't moved. His father had disappeared, venturing into the room, following the path of his wife and child's earlier escape.

Nancy was crying, and screaming, but then she abruptly stopped.

He needed to summon the strength, or more so the courage, a child of his age should never have to call upon. Getting to his feet, he inched closer to the door. The room had fallen silent now, with the light inside taking on a reddish-orange hue. The acrid smell of his own urine reached his nostrils now that he was standing and it wafted up to him as he made his way across the room. He coughed and lifted his head higher in a vain attempt to move away from his odour.

Inching closer, the house sounded like a tomb, the only noise he noted was his own shuffling, pained footsteps. Normally filled with sounds of laughter, now extinguished with the terrible events of that night.

He got to the hallway and stared down it, not wanting to see what was out of his view, inside his parent's bedroom. He hoped his family within had reconciled whatever difference had caused the breakdown of life as he knew it. He imagined the three of them, sitting on the bed cuddling and apologising, all thoughts of events prior, a long forgotten, yet painful, memory.

A smell reached him. It was almost metallic, coppery even, akin to rust.

Raising his injured arm, he held it as a fresh pulse of pain wrecked through him. Stepping into the hallway, he approached the open doorway as slowly as he could to not disturb anyone. He hoped that they were all in there, snuggled on the bed, making up for the chaos of the past few minutes. A warm embrace curing all ills that he did not want to disturb but wanted ever so to be a part of.

As he rounded the doorway, he saw his mother, lying in a pool of ever-spreading blood. Her head was facing away from him, so he could not see the frozen look of terror or the blood pouring from the gaping wound and her mouth. From his location, none of the wounds caused were visible, but the sheer amount of blood splattered throughout the room told his young mind enough of the terrifying details.

John was sitting on the bed holding Nancy, his left arm around her back to console her. To reassure her. She had stopped crying. A glimmer of hope sparked within Tom, even though his mother's fate was in front of him. He clung to any chance of normalcy but knew deep down that his life was forever damaged beyond anything resembling repair.

John was holding a large pillow that was streaked with stained blood lines in her lap and the small child's hands were below her father's arm. They seemed to have been holding on to it but now had fallen into her lap.

It was then that he saw her eyes.

Both had rolled back and upwards as the large pillow that had been held over her face had suffocated the small child. John had red scratches on the back of his hand as she had fought him with all her tiny strength against the giant of a man, but it was a fight resembling a mouse versus a bear.

John sat motionless, staring into the emptiness while Tom, who was unsure if his dad had even fully intended to kill Nancy, moved towards them both.

The knife that had killed Jane lay on the bed next to him, the dark blood was staining the sheets below it, the gold-leafed handle now fully crimson.

It was now John's turn not to see the knife.

The point of the blade easily punctured the heavy-set man's eye, popping the orb like a small water-filled balloon. It spilled the vitreous fluid down John's cheek but it wasn't long before the transparent fluid turned dark red.

Driven by anger and vengeance, the small boy had buried the blade into the man's skull as far as his strength would allow. Tom's scream gave him strength and he drove the blade further than it should have allowed, causing blood to pump from the wounded socket, the eye having been utterly destroyed.

Tom tore the knife free, only to drive it in again, and again, into his father's face. There was no rhyme or reason to the impacted area, just hatred forcing the blade's repetitious assault. Tears filled Tom's eyes as he continued to pulp the man's face, and even after John slumped back deceased, the young boy jumped up to continue his assault.

He had once loved him truly, as only a child can love a parent, unconditionally and wholeheartedly. But now, emotions were dwindling within him and a dark force drove the knife's murderous arc.

The handle had once had an intricately decorated gold trim decorating the wooden grip, but now it was so heavily stained with the familiar blood, that the pattern was mostly lost. He held it in his hands as emotions left him, leaving only malicious intent behind. The boy's remaining feelings were killed as each blow was buried deep, never to be felt again.

As the man fell to the floor, the small boy ran away.

Chapter Twelve

Cracks began appearing after the final words were uttered. The massed consciousness felt a brief respite from the crushing darkness.

As the hours ticked away, each moment became more precious, reminding them of the relentless passage of time. Time counting down carried with it a sense of anticipation and, sometimes, a touch of anxiety. It was a stark reminder that time was a finite resource, and as each movement of a clock's hands ticked by they were propelled into an even more uncertain future.

The ticking of the clock, the diminishing numbers served as poignant symbols of the ephemeral nature of existence, urging them all to make the most of every fleeting moment.

They felt that the time was coming, and they allowed themselves a moment to recover from the exertion.

"There. Isn't that better Gerald?" Came a voice from the darkness.

It wasn't directed to The All, but to the outside world. Collectively, they looked towards the voice.

"You've told a story. But you haven't got long, Gerald." Again it spoke outwards, away from everyone trapped within, yet spoke for The All.

They felt each of the words. They knew the plan.

"You have more stories. Are you man enough to tell him, Gerald?" They didn't expect a reply from the outside so continued with their diatribe which was laced with venomous intent.

Raw emotion was felt by The All. It gave them strength. Urged them all forward.

"Tell him about the love letters. The sands of time aren't on your side. These stories need to be told. Tell them to our audience before the rain stops. Tell them while you can..."

Chapter Thirteen

Gerald sat staring out of the window most days. He couldn't remember first sitting down. He couldn't even remember where the window led to.

'I've been here before,' thought the elderly man, trying to organise his thoughts.

The murky depths of the poorly maintained garden were all his vision held. It was dying and old. Like it hadn't been loved in a long, long time.

On a day like today, the old man would normally exist his way to the next sleep, spurned on by some unseen force, willing him to survive this accursed situation. He wished he would just pass, but he kept on staring out the window. Into the cursed garden.

'Death, take me.' Gerald tried to command an unseen figure, but as normal, his verbal skills failed him.

Why was it always raining as well? Every single day. Constant pouring, constant drizzle, constant storms. Constant voices around him.

He clicked back to reality as he suddenly felt different though.

Lighter somehow even.

Weights had been lifted from the world. He seemed to feel his shoulders straighten a little. He eased himself back and upright in the chair. There was no ache?

He looked around the room. There was a fellow in a police uniform sitting there with his mouth open for some reason.

This newfound independence brought strength to his

body as it did his mind and he remembered how he'd got to this point in his life.

'Sod off, you gormless idiot,' thought Gerald grumpily. Resting back into his seat, the voices quieted around him. Gerald heard a clamour behind him, noticing that a cup had been dropped earlier. It was hurriedly cleared away by the nice nurse, the one who sang. Muttered words he could not hear came from a second nurse who was scribbling notes on a clipboard. She kept glancing over and he held her gaze, trying to work out what had happened in the moments before to cause the clamour.

Settling back, he felt the brief autonomy wane and he nodded off, drifting into the warmth of a nap. His dreams brought him a vision of a garden. It had a park and families were enjoying the sun. They were happy and playful, arriving there holding hands in a blissful delight.

The sun shone down on the park users and he could almost feel the sun's warmth on his skin as he watched on ethereally.

He'd forgotten how a sunny day felt.

It rains every day now.

Chapter Fourteen

"Oh my!" I said out loud after the story finished. I wanted to say "fuck me, that was fucking epic!" but I was in uniform so 'be polite,' my instincts dictated. I try to think of the old adage that swearing is the recourse of a weak mind but fuck me, that was epic. I allowed myself one in the head because that story deserved it. Sue me.

The way the old man had told the terrible tale flowed, and I was enrapt the entire time. Literally could not tell you how long it was, didn't care much either as I could put this down as 'community engagement,' with a bit of crowbarring.

I sat there agog, as the nurses milled about cleaning up the recently smashed cup with the beverage I was not getting anytime soon. They were chatting and gesturing in Gerald's direction with that 'I know!' look on their faces. I think it was because this old codger had never uttered a word and then spilled out this story to a complete stranger. I must admit to feeling a little smug. Clearly, I have a 'tell a story to,' face. Either that or my ugly mug is a cure for dementia somehow.

It was a belter of a tale too, full of twists and turns, enigmas and mystery. He must've seen an episode of Bergerac or whatever old people watched and recounted it. Although he'd left out the part where the dashing, handsome police officer swoops in and saves the day. Midsomer mutilations! That was what Auntie Beeb was showing on endless repeat, wasn't it?

I tried to remember the story, so I could recount it to Claire when I got home, but knew I'd forget all the main points. I hastily scribbled some notes down on my trusty met notepad so I could gusto this bad boy out for the lady. What was the family name again? Knife, stabbing, chicken dinner, winner winner. It was all hastily scribbled down but I think I got the gist gisted.

Looking up, I saw that the story had taken the wind out of old boy Gerald who had nodded off. Bless his cottons. I hoped my cure would keep and he could go back to whoever he was before his brain went bye-bye.

He seemed to have a slight smile on his face too.

'He must've squeezed out a fart when I wasn't looking,' I mused, smiling at the thought, reeling at the speculated stench of death guffs. From prior dealings, old men have flatulence with a vengeance, like something had crawled up in there, made a home for itself, wife, and two kids, then tragedy had struck at the worst possible time and poof, poisonous poo poo-flavoured air.

I got up and quickly walked away from the imaginary death cloud, over to the nurse who initially greeted my entrance.

"Mel, that was something, wasn't it? I thought you said he didn't speak?" I asked interestedly. The previous nurse she was conversing with had scurried off to do something nurse-like I assume. Mel had been joined though by what I can only describe as a vulture in a cheap suit.

Mel looked away from Harpious Maximus and continued to deal with the tea/coffee calamity. This new person was an older woman with stern features, kind of like the witchy crone you'd see ruling over an orphanage with her iron fists of terror. She wore a brown suit which hid a cream blouse thing that looked like a happier colour held captive by the mean old bitch suit made of purest drab. The terracotta terror spoke to me by looking down her nose. A weird gesture as I was taller.

'Please sound like Miss Trunchbull,' I thought.

"Sorry, and you are?" Yup, bang on the money.

I realised I hadn't got anything on me that identified myself as a heroic police person so I educated her a bit. Also as a personal reminder, I must remember to badge up my shirt.

"PC Alex Chambers, SW183. At your service Ma'am." I risked smiling at her, hand out to shake, although showing her happiness might be the only justification she would need to have me locked away in the misery room. Maybe I should salute? Too much, Al, too much.

"Oh. Right. Pleased to meet you." It didn't take a Sherlock to realise that that was the dictionary definition of a 'hollow platitude,' as Croney McRestingbitchface did not seem at all pleased. Like not one little bit.

She shook my hand, the proverbial limp dead fish (hers, not mine) and I thought if I got a bit too energetic, I could have wobbled her arm off.

"Jacqueline Montgomery, head of guest services."

This, my dear, is in no way a bloody hotel, but I allowed her the piss and importance she had given herself. She's probably the only one here that's allowed to use the photocopier.

'Nothing premier about this inn,' I thought, wondering what she would say if I said that out loud.

'Orf to the misery room with this one matron!' followed by a spine-chilling cackle or a spin around the globe à la Matilda.

"Are you a relative?" She hissed, snapping my train of thought back to reality. She didn't hiss exactly, but I've already created this child catcher persona for her, so I'm running with it.

"I'm a relative of someone for sure!" Winning smile. Nope, move on. My jokes were crashing and burning today for very different reasons, but I continued because I'm just that chipper.

"No. Not of Gerald, no." I confirmed, feeling like a told-off child.

She looked at me, then back at not Uncle Gerald, and walked off, swishing a finger at Mel to clear up the tea issue, which she was anyway. She was no doubt making notes on how to kill us both. Cackle cackle.

Mel seemed to relax a bit as Madame Harridan left.

"What did you do?" She said, wanting to know. Mel gestured towards Gerald hoping for some sort of magical medical explanation.

"I don't have a magic dementia off button if that's what you're asking? Must be my winning smile!" She looked confused and I looked back at her, still fancying a cuppa. She held the parts of the broken cup she had dropped before the tale began, so would need to go back to the rubbish bin, luckily situated by the tea trolley.

"Don't you need to get that sorted?" I motioned to the broken shards in her hand in an effort to get my bloody beverage on the go. I followed her, as in ushered her like a sheepdog to the drinks trolley.

Crumbling the broken beverage beaker into the bin

she turned to speak to me again. Her back was to the tea urn. This is getting a little ridiculous now. Bag in a cup, add water, and one sugar. Come on girl!

"He's never done anything like that before. You must have a knack." And you've never made me a tea before but I'm not comparing, I concluded.

"Not sure really." I said as my '*cough* tea *cough*,' gesturing continued to hint by looking down at the unmade tea jigsaw.

"I think the doctor might need to see him," she replied, still focused on the Gezza miracle.

"Uh-huh," I muttered as I made my own bloody tea. Finally, after all this kerfuffle, the mug felt glowing in my hands.

"Got any biscuits? I could go for a chocolate hobnob after all this excitement!" I asked to the back of her head. She handed me an old tin without looking around and it was adorned with a Christmas picture where Santa was looking jolly but paint chipped. Now, it was either early or grossly late.

'This was going to need a biscuit-based risk assessment,' I deduced. Opening the musty tin, no moths fluttered out and it was without the obligatory cobweb which insinuated time passing, and I was pleased to see, at least one decent-looking nice biscuit.

"Nice by name," I said as the nurse continued to stare blankly at the snoozing Gerald. She was clearly going through some sort of medical tick sheet in her head for the old boy, so I took a biscuity bite. I'm a good judge of character and Melody was a good egg, I am however terrible at judging biscuit use by dates.

Suddenly, I regretted my life choices as the biscuit crunched wrongly in my mouth. I thought against anymore as it almost broke, cartoon style, all my teeth. The old folks must have to gum these into submission.

"I think he used to be a writer or journalist or something like that." Or just a nice old man retelling a story that popped into his head to a charming young police officer maybe?

"I fancied myself as a writer once, but found all the drafts were making me cold." She didn't even turn her head, but I knew another blank look was all over her face. Sigh. Why do I bother bringing all this sunshine?

The static crackle of my radio announced its presence nestled over near Gerald. It was still attached to the many layers that I had removed when initially sitting down.

"SW183. Receiving?" Whoops, that's me. I should probably get that, it being my job and all. I put the teacup down and trundled over to my vest to answer the chirping.

"Can you take a call in your vicinity, please? There's a job coming in to take a report about a suspicious person hanging around, near Kingston Road, shops end."

"Received, what're the details please?"

Taking down everything that was offered, I began relayering up. The coat had indeed dried out a bit which was great because it was about to get soaked again. Gerald was sitting snoring quietly in his chair so I tried to be as ninja stealthy as I had this morning, to not wake the poor old sod.

'Had a busy day haven't you champ?' I felt like giving him a reassuring hand on the shoulder but thought against it. He was a likeable old git at the end of his days and clearly using his words had knackered him out. Remembering the story again, I heard his voice. It sounded younger than I imagined. Normally old people sound as if they've been gargling sandpaper.

Dressed and not ready for the outside world, I bade Nurse Melody farewell and left, leaving the remnants of my tea behind.

The not-so-nice biscuit would now forever languish in old tin hell.

Chapter Fifteen

Duty.

Heroism.

Respect.

Those were the guiding rules for the dynamic, youthful PC sitting in the safer neighbourhoods office. He had always known he wanted to be a copper so that he could right the wrongs and catch the bad guys. So that people would give him the respect he's entitled to.

Blue lights blazing.

Suspects in cuffs.

Even thinking about it made him tingle.

It was also enough to get him up and out most days before the alarm, ready for the day's heroics.

He'd joined the met straight out of university on a fast-track sergeants course. He knew his degree in geography would help him navigate the area more efficiently and had talked his way into the job with ease. He had had no help at all from his dad, a retired superintendent, which made him proud.

With the extensive training passed, he'd joined a borough in the South of London, a leafy suburb where he could hone his craft. The local borough training commenced after meeting and greeting the senior leadership team, where he had made sure to ask them all a question to get his face out there. He'd also made sure to remind all of who his father was, in case they knew of him.

'Never hurts to drop the old man's name about for

some free respect,' thought Danny.

He knew he would ace his initial street duties course, and in doing so outperform the other recruits. They weren't his colleagues, they were a lower class of competition. He would arrest more, stop and search everyone and get results, over and above the people he was destined to lead. He would be their sergeant soon, so they should be getting out of his way in preparation for this privilege.

Respect is rank and should be shown.

After training, he was off to a safer neighbourhood team where he would learn the residential, caring part of the job. He was aiming to get out of it as soon as possible as he did not see the benefit of this. This role was for when officers were done with policing and just wanted to have tea with old women.

Danny didn't care much for that.

'No one is going to win medals for caring,' he concluded. No one ever solved anything listening to a ridiculous neighbour boundary dispute. Residents should man up and sort out their own minor shit.

He wanted Response Team.

The action...

But more so the courses!

Driving, Level Two Public Order, and then finally the pinnacle, the taser course. He wanted them all, as soon as possible. He wanted lockers filled with kits. Even if he hardly ever used it, he would order everything and be ready to pounce.

Response was where the action was. It was where he

wanted to be. Where his destiny drew him. He planned on being a skipper for a response team as soon as he was able. Not wanting to do the community-based guff that the old man assigned to him was teaching. Pointless.

He'd been dispatched to meet PC Alex Chambers on the residential road after he had been cancelled from attending a warrant. He'd been assigned to take a report of a suspicious person hanging about the area, and he planned to leave Alex doing the paperwork while he scoped the area in the SNT car he'd borrowed. Walking around patrolling is for the weak officers.

Alex was an okay guy, but was past all the excitement, past the proper policing. The subject of when Alex was retiring was a constant line of conversation between the pair, and Danny would remind Alex of his looming fate almost weekly.

This was a young man's game, and he should be moving aside.

The address in front of him was an old residential terrace. It still had the old windows which to Danny, meant that the occupant was poor. The hedge in the front was unkempt and he wanted to just leave as the person inside couldn't have seen anything of note with this mess in front of the windows.

"What a pointless call..." The young officer muttered under his breath.

The banging on the roof made Danny scream out loud, a yelp straight out of a small child. He looked out the window of the car into the rain to a smiling man, standing in the downpour.

"Bastard!" Danny barked as he opened the window

enough to get his annoyance heard. Even though the rain pelted down he could hear the guffawing laughter of his colleague.

"Come on mate," the older man said. "Let's go see what spooked this caller. Come show the young and caring side of the Met." Alex moved towards the door, still clearly chuckling.

Danny wondered why Alex gave a shit. It was probably nothing or at the very least a total load of bollocks. He hedged a bet that it was going to be a neighbour's dog that had got in his pathetic garden or some other low-level crap.

Grumbling, the young in-service officer gathered his equipment and stepped out into the rain.

Chapter Sixteen

The rest of the shift passed by without incident, and I finally got a cup of delicious tea. Twice actually, but who's counting? I needed to empty some of the unused paperwork I carry about and fill the pockets with garibaldis instead.

Plus, as an added treat I even got through lunch in the town centre. This was normally a risk as no doubt a grubby-fingered shoplifter would ruin whatever delicacy I had treated myself to.

Shoplifters were always a mixed bag. They ranged from the needy to the downright gross. Sometimes an opportunist would be added into the crime mix and if caught, automatically threw themselves under the bus as they "don't normally make bad decisions!" or it was a "spur of the moment thing!" Both would have the same look on their face though, that of 'please don't tell my mum'.

You could tell what type of thief they were by what they nicked too.

A young woman ferreting a baby powder was a different case entirely to the drug-addled meat thief, filling his grubby trousers with M&S steak. Why you would buy a defrosted grey steak from a gross dirty geezer down the pub would forever be a mystery, because it's more than likely been in his pants. Maybe not ball touchingly close, but enough to be 'eeewww'. It's really hard to brag about how you're eating ball-sack beefsteak each night whilst shitting for England because of it.

I feel sorry for most though, as generally, they're

feeling the pain of the tough times. The addict would always get the talk from me about the straight and narrow being healthier and then offering the help of the various charities that existed for just that. Even if they didn't take up any assistance, it was always worth a shot. I think I just wanted to be one of those "PC Alex changed my ways" Ted talk subjects too.

The genuinely desperate mum would get assistance in the form of stern words about crime. I would also highlight to the shop manager the time it would take for them to sort this out, adding that they would probably have to go to court too. Often this would result in a waggled finger and a despairing mum would be on her way.

Obviously, there were the more slag-baggy ones, who got the furrowed forehead of doom and my sternest of looks. I would, if so inclined, add in a 'sigh', just to ram home how much they've let down their mum.

Still, none today.

The call earlier had fizzled into nothing really, although I did have to stop Danny from both insulting the resident and calling in the flying squad. The person milling about had been a dog walker, the evidence gleaned from a local doorbell video doohickey proclaimed, but it was worth the visit as I could expound on the benefits of home security. So while nothing crime-related, help was still offered and probably accepted if I was judging his responses right.

Resident reassured, Captain Calamity and I went our different ways.

Danny soon got a body in, later that day though. I

heard him calling for extra assistance after the bloke with a single spliff 'resisted arrest'. He had obviously skipped the lesson on 'wasting police time,' and 'caution plus three,' where we'd get the person back for more stern finger waggles. Pablo Escobar had probably "apologised aggressively" which would've sent Danny into full detain mode. It was a wonder he didn't call in the police dogs or even the entirety of the British Army for his arrest of the century.

Sigh.

'He'll learn,' I mused, reminding myself to have a chat with him about it. Oh, to be young and stupid again. No, thank you. I'd rather be dashingly charming, funny and not being grilled by the custody skipper.

Shift at an end, I changed, loading my sweaty moist clothing into a bag, ready for the trip home. I've seen some officers give their greying white shirts a sniff and chuck them into the murky depths of their lockers to be used at an undisclosed time later. The emergency shirt... Exactly what reassures the public. An officer giving a death message while smelling like Hell's armpit.

'Always a clean shirt and pants at the beginning of each shift,' I recounted in my head as it was a golden rule to live by. You never knew what the day would bring, but if injured, it needs to be a 'best pants,' day. Luckily, I'd never had to flash my undies whilst injured on duty, but I knew of a few who'd been caught short.

I remember one officer was wearing his wife's pants for a bet and got into a roll-around on camera. It was the talk of the office, and while I say each to their own, the unexpected 'panting,' was a water cooler topic for quite a while. They were nice pink frilly ones too, but all I could think about was that they must be on the chafing side.

Saying my goodbyes to the team, and Danny, I prepared to leave for the boring trip home. The gung-ho hero had managed to get his body squared away by a helpful custody skipper who'd given him the 'why have you brought me this?' look and sorted the situation. Danny had left thinking he'd saved all of the Tescos globally and waited, eagerly like a puppy, for his commendation email. If only he realised that this would be classed as a day job job, and no medal ceremony was incoming.

I always looked forward to getting home, as Claire would be there. She worked at a local school as a finance officer and was allowed to work fluidly, depending on the duties needed. Since the COVID chaos of the last few years, many employers have realised that most jobs could be split between working at the office and home. It worked for Claire though as she was a workhorse, normally ending up checking on emails and other spreadsheet thingamabobs when she technically had finished. The school knew this too so let her manage her day, appreciative of her entirely.

Backs were definitely being scratched both ways so win-win. Plus the bonus for me was that she would be there, often in her comfy clothes that demanded snuggling.

I was just happy that she was happy to be fair.

I opened my terraced house door to the wafting smells of dinner. I like to play 'guess the dish,' before stepping into the kitchen. This was clearly a heat-up special from the eye of the bird's indiscriminate fish product line, which I have zero problems with, mind you. Slapping most things in between bread makes for a King's dinner in my book. Mash was my favourite. Hang on a second, mash, in bread? It is a solid gold yum. Believe me, try it. You're welcome.

Food was messing with my train of thought here. Don't worry, I'll get back to the story.

Look here it is already.

Walking into the kitchen, she was there, nose in a book, nonchalantly stirring something on the hob. I walked up to her and grabbed her around the waist, sticking my hairy mush between her and page four thousand, nine hundred and forty-seven.

I gave her a loving kiss and she recoiled playfully at the distinct aroma of the "stench of day" aftershave I wafted.

"Sod off you great bear! You stink!"

Smirking, I ruggedly cuddled into her and gave her nice rear buns a husbandly honk. Even made the noise too, because it's just the right thing to do. Her bum didn't, I did, just to be clear. I feel a 'honk honk,' always adds a positive to most squeezing situations.

She pushed me away with a real attitude of 'love you, but you smell,' and gave the giggle that always made my knees weak. I told you honking works wonders.

Leaning back, I agreed to have a shower and gave her the wink of 'come and join,' me, expressing my desire for further honking.

Dinner was overcooked and inedible. But it was worth it. She had turned everything off and rushed upstairs to join me.

I lay in bed afterwards, needing another shower. We still had it and the years of practice kept everything fresh, knowing exactly what the other needed. We had our favourite positions mind you, hers was on top, and mine was her on top, because well, boobs. Occasionally we threw in a left-field one to see if it could be added to the Chambers Sutra.

We were both spent, with the warmth of the happy afterglow still covering us. I rolled over when I could muster the energy for a snuggle, flopping my sweaty mass on her svelte one.

This was my happiest of places. She could have gone down in the garden and rolled in the cat's shit and I'd still hold her. Might be wary of where I kiss though.

"Oh God, Claire!" I blurted.

"Again?" she teased, a glint in her eye saying 'Yes. Right now. Get on it, soldier!'

"No, no, I need a recharge babe, but I've got to talk to you about an eighty-year-old man I met!"

Chapter Seventeen

I looked down at her with the glint of 'phwoar,' still in my eye but also the excitement of telling her about my day. She would always listen, even while doing other things, able to recount whatever gobbledegook I'd spluttered.

I truly felt lucky to have been with her for twenty of her forty-nine years, married for twelve of them.

We met at an old cafe by chance. I was there shovelling food into my face and she'd burst a car tire outside, rimming it one time too many times on the higher-than-normal curbs the area boasted. It was the thing of dreams for my overactive imagination and I immediately sprang to assist the damsel in distress in de street. (More chuckles to myself).

Still, one to hold doors open for, well basically everyone, I acted on heroic impulse, without realising I'd managed to get a substantial glop of food down my shirt. A hero in ketchup-stained clothes. No cape though because knowing my clumsiness, it would've got caught in the door for everyone else's benefit.

She smiled warmly back at this overweight idiot bumbling towards her but even through my oafishness, love blossomed.

'Clearly one for charity cases,' I thought at the time, but where one faltered, the other stepped in. We were made for each other. She brought out the best in me, as she was the motivation I never thought I would have. And I wanted to be better. To be as much as I could be for her.

My part mainly revolved around trying to do everything I could for her before she thought of it and I had gotten quite adept at it I might add. I can fold clean towels like a boss, and I know how to pack the dishwasher.

She gave me a purpose I never felt possible and was the one to suggest joining the police, as she said that it would fit my kind-natured spirit. I was unsure but trusted her so I set about crafting the best version of myself. Trying to get into any sort of shape, I would tell myself;

'This is to pass the job-related fitness test,' But who was I kidding? It was all for her. She asked, and she got.

Now, at 49, I was in the best shape I had ever been and intended to stay that way. When I say best shape, I mean 'probably not going to die imminently due to being a fatty fatty fat fat,' and I also didn't want to be a crush hazard in the bedroom department.

Knowing what was coming fitness-wise in the job application, I also started working on my stamina levels. It was initially to catch the naughty criminals, but it had the bonus of keeping the motion in the ocean going without me having a heart attack mid-thrust. Solid win-win there.

I felt healthy and alive and wanted to keep it that way because each day with Claire was the reason for everything.

Even down to the minutiae of beard length.

Claire preferred the facial fuzz longer as when I trimmed it down to whatever design I could be bothered with, she would take great joy in telling me how wonky it was. I'd then spend an hour trying to line up everything until all I was left with was a poorly aligned soul patch.

So why bother trying to be hip and trendy?

I say hip and trendy, I would normally copy whatever movie superhero had the most sex appeal.

'Same beard, same appeal,' I would try to convince myself. I just didn't come with the same cash levels or actual sex appeal.

'I've got Batman's powers and Spiderman's money,' Even I chuckled to myself at that one, and as Claire was still with me, I must have something appealing. My guess was my absolutely enormous, totally amazing sense of humour.

She completely and utterly sidetracked me.

But she was worth it.

And was still lying there waiting for a story about an octogenarian.

Chapter Eighteen

"He told you a story?" Claire uttered as their after-sex conversation revealed more details. Normally they wouldn't chat for a while as Alex tended to have the worst post-nuptial sex talk.

Claire felt a bit deflated after her husband's initial cry of 'Oh God,' as she could've easily had sex again as enough time had passed in her opinion. She loved this man. Their love made everything better, including the sex. He was eager to please her and he often did, through words alongside actions.

Ever since she first saw him and his bumbling attempts to woo her, she knew they'd be together forever. Her heart was ready and open for an oaf of such loving magnitude. He had a heart that overflowed for her, and she reciprocated totally. Even though it was a tacky sentiment, they completed each other.

She would always welcome his cuddle as his ergonomic form touched her, moulding themselves together in love and safety. She used to think it gross to hug a sweaty person but with him, it didn't matter. She wanted to be touching him always.

"Yes, he did! And it was a doozy. Come on, let's eat. I've got to tell you all about Gerald! Oh, and how I cured dementia!" He was almost giddy with excitement as he rushed back to the shower for a quick rinse-off. She smiled at the sight of his bare arse and considered joining him again, but they'd end up in a never-ending cycle, unbreakable until one of them died.

He was such an easy pull though. All she had to do was start changing in front of him and he'd be all over her. He was most definitely a 'boob man,' which he often self-proclaimed to her. Whenever she was feeling amorous, she'd use her much-loved weapons against his minimal defences.

Claire smiled. She heard the shower turn on and a brief whimper as the cold water hit the overly eager man. The mental vision of her man leaping out of the waterfall and squealing in protest brought a smile to her face. She was still chuckling at the mental image as the water warmed. She then took to imagining him slopping lynx shower gel everywhere, hurriedly covering all the worst offending areas. He still used the African variety of the popular shower gel for some ungodly reason, which was odd as he was far removed from a sixteen-year-old teenager off out clubbing.

Alex headed downstairs to rescue dinner, throwing on his old blue towelling robe as he clumped down each stair, leaving Claire to freshen up in peace.

The hot water felt glorious on her still tingling body. Each rivulet of water seemed to wash away all stress, leaving only a feeling of ease. She could've stayed there longer but she could hear Alex crashing about getting their food prepped.

Throwing on some easy lounge clothes she headed downstairs, and Alex smiled as they passed in the hallway to the kitchen and managed a skilful 'woohoo,' alongside an open robe flash whilst carrying his dinner.

"Silly twat," she mused happily.

"Your's is in the microwave." He said as she watched his head disappear from view.

He was competent enough, but she liked to finish the

jobs she had started, knowing that he was more active in his day job than her mathematical accounting. He was having none of it though and wanted to share all the tasks, even take on more so that she didn't have to.

"Both full-time jobs though babe," Alex would say, but Claire wanted to help him as much as he helped other people.

Grabbing her food which was luckily still hot, she went to his side in the living room. Long gone were their days of sitting at the table staring into each other's eyes. They were both happy with the sitting-on-the-sofa eating regime that now dominated dinner. Afterwards, she would normally pop her feet under Alex to warm them and have contact with him.

Alex began his tale even as he stuffed food into his mouth. He was starving after the day's and more recently evenings,' actions, but desperate to tell her about his day and the story he was regurgitating. She would listen intently to him, not even caring about the content, just happy to be hearing the story told with such gusto. The tale started with him giggling at the word moist a lot and then moved effortlessly to an old man opening up to him. Blushing, he got to the part of the story where a man discovered his wife in a secret tryst with another woman. He went on, through the terrible tale of the boy Gardener who had survived a terrible father. His recitation was an emotional rollercoaster, filled with highs and terrible lows.

He finished, waiting for her response eagerly like a child explaining the details of their favourite toy.

"So you spent most of the shift listening to an old man?" She teased, knowing that that was not the response he craved. Claire waited for the retort to blurt back as he always missed her little devil's advocated jabs. Purely playful, but always missed.

"Claire!"

She laughed.

'Got him again', she thought.

"Yes, it was a good story. Well done for making a connection with him. Probably helped him a great deal. What did the staff say though? Were they pissed?" She wanted to know. Alex then went into great detail in regards to what he described as 'the tea incident', and Claire listened again, hanging on to each of his words.

He did have a way with people, which is why she had suggested, against her own better judgement, joining the police. She knew he'd be an excellent officer, able to help anyone through anything. But she hated the idea that her yang could be in any sort of danger. Claire knew that having him in that role was a benefit to the very society she thrived in, as he could bring the same happiness she felt to others more in need.

Every moment to her was a risk to her very completion as his loss would cripple her beyond repair.

The evening continued after the massacred dinner, with them lying on the sofa together. The cod in batter was essentially fossilised by the time they got to it, but Alex was too excited with his anecdotal adventure to mention it. He never would to her either as he was happy to eat anything provided with love.

As they relaxed, Claire had her head in her book, whilst Alex lay alongside her watching his crime shows. He was deep into season 'too many,' of a cold case program, hosted by a failed actor in his twilight years.

Something was nagging at her though. There was a feeling gnawing at the base of her skull. This annoying knot plagued her, distracting her from her novel, the frustration already making her repeat multiple pages of the prose in front of her. Looking away from the page, she took stock of the issue.

There was something wrong with the story that Alex had told.

There was something there that drove her to replay it, repeating sections over and over, hoping the repetition would cause a synapse link of understanding.

There was something...

She furrowed her brow as if the motion would cause the understanding she sought as her analytical mind needed to crunch the numbers, to work through the details he had mentioned in the search for the source of the nag. She thought she had heard parts of it somewhere before, but some of the details, the essence of the tale were slightly off though.

She ticked through things she had seen and heard before, retelling tales from books past to match the details explained earlier. Images flowed through her mind and she swiped them away when they weren't what she sought.

She had heard this story before.

But where...?

Chapter Nineteen

Gerald sat staring out…

'Have I said all this before? This isn't me,' thought the old man as he squirmed in his chair. The respite was brief though and the moment of clarity was crushed back down within him.

Gerald sat staring out of the window most days. He couldn't remember sitting down or even leaving the chair. What day was it?

"It's the same day Gerald. Over and over." came a voice.

He looked around but saw no one in the room.

He thought he saw the outline of a figure in the corner of his vision, but he blinked and rubbed his face with a weak bony hand. He was alone with just his thoughts.

"You're going to suffer, Gerald."

He closed his eyes, reopening them to try and focus on the expansive venue. With failing eyesight, he couldn't see clearly into the hobby room further than a few feet, but he was sure that no one was in vocal range to speak to him. The care staff knew he was losing his hearing and all his faculties, so would lean in and enunciate every syllable, holding his sight line to show him that they were talking to him. They often placed a hand on his shoulder too for added comfort.

"You're going to tell all your stories, Gerald. All of them. I'm going to make you."

Gerald sank back in his high-backed chair and hoped the voice would disappear. If he pressed himself into the upholstery, no one could see him. He'd be safe.

The threats were too clear in his mind to be from a source within the four walls.

'Go away!' He thought to say it out loud but again was brought back to the same point as he always found himself.

Gerald sat staring out of the window most days. He couldn't remember...

'What? What's going on?' He suddenly realised that he had just thought those very words about staring out of the window. They were known to him off by heart it seemed and he concluded that his mind was stuck in a loop brought on by his desperate loneliness and utter despair.

Realising that it was all in his head, it must be there, he knocked on his temple to try and shake off the feeling. His weak arms barely managed the task though as he felt a sudden change within himself.

He began to feel a biting cold, deep within his bones, his internal temperature plummeting. He pulled the robe tighter around himself, but the temperature was falling in him, not the room. The feeble attempt to heat himself failed as the chill clawed up from his core, spreading through his body. Each thud of the clawed ethereal hand hit him as the bitter, glacial chill spread throughout his body.

Was it time? Yes. He began to welcome the feeling, aware that this was his last moment. He smiled, wanting the abyss to take him.

"Not yet, you bastard."

He whimpered at the sentence, his moment of clarity suddenly washed away, like love letters written in the sand.

Gerald sat staring out of the window most days. He couldn't remember first sitting down. Couldn't even remember where the window led to.

It was outside. Where though, he didn't know that either.

At least he was warm in his comfy chair.

On a day like today, he'd pass the time away, watching the rain fall.

"That's better Gerald. That's where I want you. Confused, dazed, and alone," came a voice. The old man twisted around and saw a young woman. She was in her thirties, with long black hair cascading down her shoulders. It would have had bounce and life to it, had it not been covered in dried blood, matted to the white floral dress.

In the centre of her chest, a gaping hole of darkness drew him in, the feeling of terror quickly rising in him. He moved his hand to his crotch instinctively to try to stop himself from uncontrollably urinating.

"How you laughed when I cried, each time I saw the tide..." The woman smiled with a hideous, disfigured grin as it spoke the words. Out of context, it sounded like poetry or a reading at a wake.

He closed his eyes, tears falling down his cheeks.

He wished that today, like most days, would end.

*

This time, the darkness welcomed The All. They knew

that time was catching up to Gerald.

The eagerness within them all was felt throughout. They wanted the stories told, with the second one coming. Not today though as they did not want to tire out the old bastard.

"You're ours until we send you to hell."

They smiled.

As one.

Chapter Twenty

Another day, another dollar.

That's one of the most annoying sayings ever in my book. Firstly, because we get paid in pounds. Secondly, what if it was a day off? What do I say then? No one's going to pay me for sitting on my arse watching the telly and I'm certainly not asking for a wage slip for doing the chores, that's just helping.

The things I think about whilst on the loo, version four hundred and eighty-seven.

Yesterday's dinner had not been kind to my digestive system as the overly crunchy cod and mushiest of broccoli were not a delicacy that's going to catch on in house Chambers. The preparation was fun, don't get me wrong...

I'd got up and ready earlier that morning as the rumbles in my stomach woke me from a blissful sleep. Cannot remember my dreams, but I was probably doing something overly heroic and days were saved. Pre loo, I'd got up and ready, dressed to earn another pound in another shift. (That's not going to catch on either. I'll brainstorm something out later).

Work then beckoned, the second early shift of a set of three. I wasn't much of a morning person because I'm not a psychopath and thought about the seven a.m. start. The timetable was clearly designed by someone who would never have to work it, which is why I was squeezing out my disliked dinner at just before six.

Open window, check, match lit, check check.

'This will need some fabreezing too,' I thought, making

sure the air was rose based for Claire later on. I don't know why, but whenever I went in after her, the entire toilet was always cleaner than before she went in. She must sit there with an extendo-mop cleaning while crapping. She doesn't even take in a book or newspaper or Nintendo Switch!

The mind boggles.

*

The office was a hubbub of activity when I arrived with Danny regaling the team of his heroics of yesterday. I don't think anyone was listening but he kept tapping people on the arm as if to say 'Wait till you hear what happened next!' He was going to go over the whole rigmarole of it all, so I decided to tune out the utter bollocks he was spouting.

"You did your day job then?" said an officer as he passed through the room. He'd stopped to use our photocopier as all the others in the building were broken. Or to put it in clearer terms, had run out of paper. Danny muttered under his breath and continued talking to whoever was not listening.

I don't think he realised that we already knew everything as we all have the same radio network as him. Upon his more units call though, we all intently listened as we made our way to help our overzealous colleague. The skipper though had been in a partner's meeting and only got wind of the shenanigans after the custody skipper had squared it away. He'd changed to the spare channel on the way to the cells in Wandsworth with his miscreant and the custody skipper had torn him a new one for wasting more time. Danny was unaware that I, alongside probably the entire South West Basic

Command Unit had switched also and heard the tirade.

If police officers were anything, they are all nosy curtain twitchers. Like your nan, but in uniform. Scratch that vision immediately, sorry about that. Being inquisitive kind of goes with the job to be fair to us. If we weren't and didn't poke and nose, no crime would ever get solved. This inquisitorial nature brought with it a healthy dose of the 'uh-huh,' when a scallywag was telling clear pokies.

Sergeant Wilson was on yesterday and wasn't one to suffer foolish police officers gladly. She was an utter tyrant, a proper scary boss who would storm literally everywhere. I've never known anyone to walk at all times with clenched fists. And yesterday, I imagined the back of her neck pulsating with fury as she was trying to keep her volcanic temper in check, even whilst she was telling him how to do things correctly and not the same way he'd seen on the television. She was explaining to this puppy of a police officer how it could've, should've been handled, in the full knowledge that her audience was larger than just Dan.

Danny was having none of it though this morning. He was the hero of Kingston in his eyes. This one arrest had solved not only all our sleepy borough's woes but also brought euphoric world peace. There was a light behind his eyes as the ceremony of commendation played out behind them.

It was going to be a long day.

'More shit per shift,' I thought, careful to keep my sweary words internal. I was not looking forward to the day ahead, especially as it looked like rain again.

*

The doorway to the backyard looked greyer and more foreboding than normal. I had hoped to get a lift to the far end of the ward so I could crisscross my way back home on foot. My aim today was to stick to the back roads to do some reassurance walks. This meant that I would walk up and down roads with my radio on so that the residential curtain twitchers would spread the word that they actually saw a police officer today.

We often had complaints that 'we never see you!' and that we should deploy more officers. Well, we don't see you either and unless you're looking out of your window twenty-four seven, you're not going to know we were there. Grumble grumble. Pet hate rant there. Obviously, all officers would like more bobbies on the beat, but times were hard and we had to work with what we had. (Left).

I was working myself up into a lather before anyone had even said anything to me when the bearded hulk walked past again.

"Morning!" I said as chirpily as my grumps would allow.

Clearly, English was not his first language and he gruffed a hello back in runic viking. I believe it was in the tongue used by the bearded barbarians of old. Should I point out that he's left his battle axe and shield?

"Off to ransack Surbiton?" I joked. So many jokes to choose from…

He looked around, confused by my random chain of words. I waved and he continued to stomp toward his vehicle. If I see him tomorrow, I'm going to converse in rune stones, but more to the point, I'm not getting a lift from him, I concluded.

My left boot resigned to movement and I stepped out into the yard, nodding hello's to the known faces gathered.

On the slower days, I spin things through my head to pass the time. Today was a continuation of my toilet time wonderings of earlier, as I was still trying to come up with a replacement saying for the dollar/pound issue. I liked things that had multiple meanings, so I tried to add in an acronym so that it was pre-approved by the police's marketing department. I thought that some of the higher-ups conversed in a form of verbal acronym language, known only by the police elite.

Chuckling, I found my boots had brought me to a familiar doorway.

Shady Oaks care home stood before me.

A familiar face looked out through sunken eyes.

Morning Gerald.

Chapter Twenty-One

It was a day like most others. He'd sit there, staring out, into the rain. His striped pyjamas were fresh on and had the faint smell of cheap lavender, having been washed by the cleaning crew yesterday. He was still able to wash and dress himself but as he wasn't going to leave the elderly prison, pyjamas were all that were needed.

The world was crushing today. As was every day now. There was a sense of clarity every so often in recent days. Much like now.

He somehow remembered the doctor saying that moments of clarity in dementia patients meant the end was near. And strangely, he was fine with that. He was accustomed to death and was ready. Willing its approach even.

He was bringing his life back into the brightness now as images of everything he'd ever done, all his achievements, and his fond memories were coming back into focus. He remembered his family, his loves, and his work. The memories would drift and merge though as they reorganised themselves from a lost library.

His once methodical, calculating mind was reclassifying his life into a cogent order.

*

It was too soon. They all thought that they had time.

He was remembering. They felt strength returning too. The darkness awoke and knew that his awareness could not be allowed to happen yet. There was more to be done.

Not now, Gerald. Back in your box.

Chapter Twenty-Two

Gerald sat staring out of the window most days. He couldn't remember first sitting down. Couldn't even remember where the window led to.

He was in the same chair as always, wearing the same old pyjamas.

He liked being here, it felt safe. He told himself that every day.

In the sunlit room that he must've lived in for decades, he sat, and his face bore the wrinkles of time and wisdom. He had long ago accepted the life sentence at the care home, and through the years, he'd become a contented resident. He found solace in the simplicity of his existence, having discovered a freedom of the mind that transcended the physical constraints of his surroundings.

He kept reminding himself that he was content in the richness of his world. But he knew that he had a story to tell, and he longed to tell it.

Gerald looked out of the window and an officer was standing there. The policeman strode up the worn path towards the door of the reception, where further beyond, he would hear his story.

He liked telling tales.

Gerald felt a complete compulsion, against all strength, to talk to this officer. He needed to get the story off his chest, to divulge his tale to the police.

'When he gets here, we'll tell the story,' thought Gerald eagerly.

Chapter Twenty-Three

Melody was nowhere to be seen. There was a pleasant girl at reception today who was built mainly of smiles. Even when talking, she kept up the facade, grinning from ear to ear which either said, 'I'm pleasant and helpful all the time!' or 'I'm out on day release. Can I use your scissors?'

"I don't have scissors," I said to her unthinkingly.

She looked at me, clearly not computing what relevance that had on anything due to my train of thought verbalising my nonsense. I really should think before I do anything. Especially in regards to scissors.

"Never mind. Thinking out loud." I said. There. Sorted. Kind of.

She ushered me into the lobby hobby room, or whatever it was called, as she tried to make sense of the cutting remark from earlier.

"One sugar in mine please," I said hoping the sledgehammer hint would be picked up. Nothing could go wrong now I had brought the conversation back down to beverage-based requests.

Tina. Again, I made sure to check the name badge, not the boobage. She was quickly becoming my new favourite as she flicked the large water drum to its heat setting. She was complying with my request in her quest to help everyone with everything. This confirmed to me that she was indeed manically customer service-based and not just manic.

She made a killer tea too.

Waiting for the tea to get to the correct colour before

adding the milk, I glanced over at Gerald and as before, the weird old sod was watching me.

Hang on old timer, be there soon.

Checking for dunkables, I only saw sad Santa again so thought better of it. 'Biscuit-free but with tea,' was acceptable for how today was going.

At least I was getting a tea pre-story this time. It would help settle into whatever he was going to divulge today, because, if it was anything like the last beast of a book, I would be in for another doozy.

Moving over to the old guy, Tina click-clacked her way back to the desk to serve a delivery person who'd wheeled in a trolley load of boxes. One was marked with the telling 'McVities,' logo so it would hopefully soon be biscuit o'clock.

"Morning mate. How are you feeling today?" I began the task of stripping off again so that I didn't have a bad back later on. Plus it gets a bit musty and it's also difficult to sit properly with the Metvest pushed up under my nose.

'Must be how Dolly Parton feels,' I thought.

Besides it's Gerald for fuck's sake. Or is it for fuck sake? Who is fuck? Whoops, tangent again. I'm going off on more than one today, and not as focused as normal.

"Do you want to have a chat today?" I offered him the chance to actually converse and not just narrate something wonderful. Might be nice to find a bit out about him. Maybe he would want to know about me! I'm an interesting guy you know.

"You made a vow, that you, would ever be true," said

Gerald.

Nope, straight into the story.

I settled into the chair and brought the tea up to my lips, eager to hear this new tale. I fancied one about spaceships if I was being honest.

Gerald looked at me sternly as if knowing my head was all over the shop, so I shrugged and brought myself back into the real world.

Here we go again.

Helen's Heart

A short story by Gerald Heggarty

1

"You made a vow, that you, would ever be true," crackled out of the record player as Helen swung her hips to the music. Her eyes were closed as the lyrical voice of Pat Boone crooned his tune for the dancing woman. The words filled her as she listened, head held back as her long dark hair flowed and swayed with her movements.

Each sashay brought a new swing to the long floral dress she wore. Her movements were tidal, a swagger that wafted back and forth.

She felt his eyes on her as the chorus began. He was standing in the doorway to their small laundry room, watching her every move.

Smiling, she turned around to see the man she had married.

He was a slight man, but it was his intellect that had attracted her in the first place. His mind was an alive darting beast, always calculating each weary step. Attracted was the wrong word though as she had not thought of him sexually, or even lovingly at any point in time. She reasoned with her parents that this man was of money, or would at least bring her the status she craved.

Oliver was lead editor at the local newspaper which brought standing. Living in the area also added to his appeal as Bournemouth was an ever-growing, bustling seaside town. Visitors flocked to the bustling beach to visit the pier for two and a half pence, or a trip via boat to other equally gorgeous towns. Fish and chip wrappers would fill and clutter the beaches each day much to the chagrin of all the residents, their leftover morsels hunted by scavenging animals.

Status was all Helen cared about though, caring not for this man standing in front of her. He would be able to get her out of town and to London, as she constantly pushed him to get a better job in the city. Once there she would have the run of the town and leave Oliver to his work, while she played and cavorted.

She was considered a plain girl, not one with the stunning movie star look of the seventies. Her long dark hair was a good look on her though and she would flick and play with it to entice her prey. It bordered her slim face which seemed to lengthen it further and highlight the dark brown pools of her eyes. She was slender and not at all full of figure which was lusted after by most men, so when Oliver showed interest, and she found out he had appropriate community standing, she set about capturing him.

They would marry, then possibly gift him one child, and after, get rid once she had everything she could squeeze out of him. She would wring him dry as a husk before tossing him aside for the next ladder rung.

Oliver was carrying a laundry basket loaded to the brim with neatly folded linen and clothing. She had told him to do a full load once he returned from work and he had dutifully obliged. But something was wrong. She would find it.

"You've folded the sheets incorrectly Oliver. Sort it out, Oliver." She demanded.

He sighed and returned to the laundry room to readjust his task.

"Don't you sigh at me, Oliver. You brought this on yourself. You should have done the job the correct way in the first place."

He had completed the task with the due diligence of a master craftsman, but she felt the need to alter her exact instructions on a whim. She mused that this would keep even the meagrest of tasks problematic at best, arduous or even torturous at worst.

Helen returned her attention to the record and put the song on once more. She enjoyed the melodious voice of Pat Boone ever since a young age, but his crooning was another part of her plan since Oliver was not one for music. She would often play the same song multiple times because she knew he liked to watch her move, but the repetition never allowed him to truly be free and enjoy the moment.

Everything she did was a drip drip drip.

'But somehow, that vow, meant nothing to you', crooned the music as she swayed to the rhythm, eyes closed and smiling.

*

In the small laundry room, Oliver kept silent. He was thinking about how to change his situation. Permanently.

2

Oliver carried out his husbandly duties without fuss or complaint. He strove for a quiet life, to never be noticed. He had chosen Helen for her plainness so that she wouldn't stand out in the crowd. A wallflower to his solitary darkness.

A wife had completed the facade of him and at the beginning, he thought that they could be happy. She had drawn him in with a playful flick of her hair and, for one moment, he thought happiness may be gifted to him. It had been a long time since he had felt anything at all, and he knew that feelings were a risk.

A troubled past had made him cautious. Never knowingly wanting to stand out from the crowd. He worked to keep his appearance an afterthought, so no one would remember this beige man, occupying no space in the world. His presence was always a footnote in the corner of your eye.

He liked it that way. It was a craft he had mastered over time. Honed to perfection, he was a nobody in clothing, a shadow forgotten.

Working his way up to editor was part of the plan so that he could work in the background without being in the spotlight. He would task others, and let them lead but just work enough to get by.

Nobody could know who he was.

Not even Helen.

She had married him later than the norm, and in their mid-twenties had become man and wife in a small registry office just outside of town.

It was a happy day. Oliver had even risked a glimmer of hope.

Helen was surrounded by friends and family, and Oliver had a small handful of work colleagues. His parents had died years before so could not walk him down the aisle, but Stewart from Legal filled the best man role to perfection.

No stag do or parties were arranged by the solicitor at Oliver's request. He did not drink as a defence to keep his guard up and not reveal truths hidden, and parties were very public gatherings.

Helen on the other hand had spectacle after spectacle. Each party was louder than the last. A brash event extravaganza to nurse her overly inflated ego, but it kept her happy.

'A right carry-on,' he had thought at the time but such palaver helped to keep Oliver hidden away in the background.

The years that followed darkened though as she seemed to become picky and bitter. Each task pushed Oliver more and more internally, to protect his feelings and sanity. Everything he was ordered to do had to be completed to an exact blueprint, and even when perfect, still errors were found. Nothing was ever simple at home. The smallest of tasks were declared wrong and had to be redone from scratch to fit exacting, and often unknown, guidelines.

It was one of the reasons he had taken to not saying anything. He just read his books and planned his thoughts.

Nightly, she would listen to the radio, or play records while her aspirations of being a dancer played out to the music. 'Love letters in the sand,' was a staple of almost every night. He knew it word for word, note by note. He could even pick out where the record has a slight crackle, distorting the singer's melody, ever so slightly. The lyrics had even slipped into his writing and he had been pulled up multiple times by proofreaders for saying 'on a day like today,' in more than one article. Even they would offer suggestions on what to say.

She was entrancing to watch though. He was still attracted to her, even while she held back their lovemaking as punishment if his tasks were wrong. That was the pain that hurt the most. While she was not forthcoming with romance or even the odd compliment when he was inside her, he felt the closeness he desperately needed.

At that moment, he did not care for anything she said or did, he was warm and safe. He was trying to be cautious, but he wanted so desperately to love and be loved. His heart screamed out to be filled with warmth once again, so settled for other comforts a woman could bestow. He had not felt cherished or adored since his mother passed away many years previous. He wanted to be held, be comforted.

But comfort brought risk.

Risk means exposure.

He thought his initial plan was best, to stay quiet and hidden.

Even though the woman he felt a glimmer of love for was also his captor and tormentor.

*

Months passed and Oliver's situation only grew darker. He'd grown accustomed to getting up earlier each day and leaving the house before she was awake to miss the deluge of abuse that spewed forth with her waking moments. He would walk the streets, sometimes in darkness, with just his thoughts.

Sometimes he would arrive early to work, and stay later, making excuses that gave a brief respite from the torrential abuse. The debasement would begin anew though when he had to step foot across the threshold of what should have been his castle.

Each day would darken both his mood and demeanour, a pitch-black weight making his existence all the more cimmerian in nature.

Given his history, it was not a place to dwell.

3

As the months rolled on, Helen grew to hate Oliver. The mere sight of him set her tempers flaring. His constant subservience would grate on frayed nerves and she could not fathom how he took such abuse.

Most of her waking hours were spent planning new and more excruciating torture tactics to impose upon the man. She had taken to asking the impossible and he had complied, even though she could see it hurt him. Mundane tasks became convoluted to the point where even simple things like putting away cutlery became a labyrinthine assignment.

Still, he complied without raising his voice or hand.

On one occasion she had made him prepare, bake and serve an apple pie from scratch for her book club and had thrown it at him because the striated decoration on the crust was in the wrong direction. She had not held back either. The steaming desert had hit him in the chest, splattering him and sending him back a step. The gathered guest's muffled laughter was a mix of shock and disgust, but to Helen, it was worth it. She had an audience, and more importantly, witnesses.

She wanted him to break, to lose control and run away, or better still to kill himself so that she could play the grieving wife. A spouse left with all of Oliver's wealth.

She knew he had money, as whenever she asked for anything, it appeared without complaint. She just didn't know where exactly he kept it. She could see his wage packet each month because she would take the notification slip from him and check it over.

But she knew he had more squirrelled away. How and where he got it though was a mystery. A conundrum that would be answered easily with his death.

It was tiring though, thinking of a new argument each night. It had got to the point where she was rehashing old issues that Oliver had dealt with, purely so that she could continue her campaign of hate-filled abuse.

Still, he kept silent though. Only speaking when spoken to, and never raising his voice. He took everything she threw at him, both literally and figuratively.

She needed something else. Something to finally push him over the edge.

She ran scenarios through her mind, ticking off the ones she had used before, mentally remembering the ones that had the most impact.

She stopped her thought process on something she hadn't tried before. This was a new form of torment and needed planning, so it would have the most impact. This would be the punch she needed to send him over the edge once and for all.

She would hit him hard with this new torture.

Their family.

4

The winter had crept in quickly that year. Storms had lashed the south coast, making the years normally bountiful beaches a no-go area. Businesses had suffered. Tourists kept away. Even the most foolhardy stalwart of visitors found it difficult to justify the trip.

Then a brief few days of sunshine, brought with it a horde of people, filling each scenic spot to the brim, their rubbish piling high. Residents vocalised their disgust at the litter issue while local businesses raked in the cash they missed from the previous bad weather season.

Helen had planned this out to perfection. Got the timing of the day right. It was in place for the evening. She tingled with excitement at the thought of finally being free of this man she was lumbered with.

She would push him to his edge and then crush his spirit, throwing everything he loved off a cliff, into the murky depths below.

Oliver returned from work later than usual and she chose to not shout at him for it. Instead, she cooked dinner. She had made his favourite, bangers and mash. It was simple, like him, which was probably why he liked it so much. She'd even taken the time to fry off the onions for the gravy so that he knew it was going to be a special night.

Part one was to lull him into a false sense of security.

They ate and Helen, while not caring, asked about his day. Oliver was taken aback and unsure of where she was going but dutifully answered. They were conversing like a regular couple, and at one point, he even managed a smile.

"Oliver, I need to tell you something. I know things have been tough, but it's only because I want the best for you." A lie, but worth it.

He looked up from his food and mopped his mouth of the thick gravy, dabbing at both cheeks with the napkin.

"I know you've always wanted a family. I have too, but we've never seemed to be able." Part two was being set up in front of him and he was unaware. She looked coyly down at her stomach, the beginnings of a playful grin starting to appear on her face.

"Well I spoke to Doctor Gardener this morning and he confirmed we are having a baby!" She raised her voice at the end to feign excitement, smiling as hard as she could. It was actress in quality and she knew it had worked.

His face lit up, and all darkness lifted.

Facial muscles that had not moved in years finally sprung to life. He burst into joyous tears and stood up hurriedly, moving to her side. He clutched her, holding her tightly with an embrace of warmth and emotion. His embrace suddenly ended though as he thought to not hold her too tightly, placing one hand delicately on her stomach.

She hugged him back and reciprocated the embrace, realising that this was allowed at this time in her pregnancy. Helen relaxed into the hug as best she could and although he was stronger than she remembered, melded herself into the embrace. They held each other for moments that felt eternal as Oliver said in her ear,

"Thank you."

*

He could not remember feeling this way. His initial shock at hearing her words had given way to a warmth his heart yearned for. His core longed for a family and this would change everything. Yes, he would still keep the same discretion and secrecy going, but he would have a child who would love him unconditionally.

He would protect his young child with the strength born of parenthood, the baby's protection was now his life's work. His mind began prepping for every outcome, every mood swing hormones could bring, every ask that would arrive. Everything would be perfect because he would make it so.

Oliver's mind was alive with everything that crossed it. Hope began to break the surface of his desolation.

Nothing would hurt them, or him, again.

5

"On a day like today, we passed the time away, writing love letters in the sand" crooned out over the record player as the happy couple danced in each other's arms.

Oliver remembered this at their wedding years ago, this same feeling. The swaying warmth as the music filled you, holding your loved one in your arms. It was what life was supposed to be about. This was the done thing because it was right and true.

Even though he hated this song, they were dancing and it was a step in the right direction. Gone were the harsh words. The criticisms now seemed a thing of the past. All he could think about was this moment and he risked allowing happiness in.

"Let's go to bed." Helen purred in his ear.

She held his hand as they left the room, her leading as they moved to the stairs. Lights were being flicked off as they went, closure on their lives previous. Oliver moved to the stairs to assist her up, even though at this early stage such caution was unwarranted.

Outside the storm continued to rage blowing the gale around them, but at that moment, Oliver cared not.

*

Helen was giddy with excitement. Not for the same reason as Gerald, but for the incoming heartbreak. The hammer was to fall exactly as planned.

Each step filled her with fresh waves of joy as they neared the bedroom. The landing light blazed into life as Oliver turned to look upon the new face of their new relationship, their lives beginning anew.

She noticed him smiling broadly as if the years of punishment never happened. His face was still tear-stained as the emotion of the evening filled him.

The cream walls lined her plan. The hallway was where she would break him. There, as they stood facing each other on the plush fitted carpet, would be the end. She would finally be free of this subservient rat-faced little man. Free to live her life as the grieving widow who had sadly lost her husband.

She readied herself. This would be the moment he broke, and she imagined him hanging himself from the light fitting to her left. She'd awake in the morning with mock shock at the sight of his corpse.

Helen prepared the biggest lie she would, could ever tell.

"Are you sure you are alright with raising another man's child though?"

6

"Oh. Did I not mention it?" She continued.

He looked as if he'd been punched hard in the stomach, physically and not just figuratively. Her words had the desired impact. He even stumbled back a step as the wind seemed to be forced from him with the violent emotional hammer blow.

She had hurt him.

To his very core.

She had won.

"Yes, Oliver. The baby isn't yours. I wish I knew who it was though, so we wouldn't have all this kerfuffle."

She watched as her words crushed the man before her, the colour running from his cheeks. She savoured the last few words like a fine wine. She tasted his pain in the air. She wanted more. Each sentence she had written placed Oliver in a mock boxing match, each word a jab here, a left hook there.

"You didn't think it was yours though did you? I mean we haven't had sex in as long as I can remember. Not anything near good sex anyway."

She watched as her words continued their gut punch through the now crushed man in front of her.

Tears began flooding down his cheeks as he spluttered and crumbled.

This was what she had hoped for.

She would be free.

Oliver was hunched over now, barely able to keep standing. He took a step toward Helen, but it faltered as he saw that the woman in front of him could not hold back her smile any longer. 'Time to ram the pain home', she thought.

"Well I am sorry that you thought it was yours. You really should clarify what is happening, Oliver. You only have yourself to blame."

It was like a one-two punch, over and over to the destroyed man. Each word was carved into his brain, forever to torment him. He would never feel anything, ever again, lost to endless despair.

He raised his arms to hold her, more so to be held, his emotions snapping and collapsing under each word his wife uttered. He needed this to end, the pain to leave him.

She laughed at such a pathetic gesture and said,

"Don't be so silly, Oliver. Why would I want to touch you?"

The moment stopped in time.

He was standing in front of her, hunched over, a broken man.

And then his past caught up with him.

7

She did not realise Oliver was taller than she was. He'd always been hunched over with the weight of the world slumping him earthward. Now, he was standing at full height, a full foot taller than her.

The light in his eyes was gone.

Tears had stopped.

His face was emotionless.

He reached up, placing both hands on her shoulders, and threw her downstairs.

*

Her eyes blinked.

All she could see was white.

Lights flashed as her senses came back to her.

Pain rushed up her arm as she tried to raise her head.

She couldn't move.

She couldn't talk.

Her mind raced as the situation gradually came into focus. The white she was seeing was the ceiling, the pain in her arm from her left hand.

She took stock of the situation. She felt cold, a draft coming in from somewhere. Helen knew at that moment that she was naked. Trying to get up, the horror of her current situation hit home as the rope binding her to the table stung under the tightly knotted bindings.

Panic streaked through her mind. She was gagged, naked, and bound to the dinner table. Unable to lift her head, she tried to turn it to see what damage was causing the throbbing pain pulsing up her arm. She could not see clearly, but knew the two fingers, pointing at unnatural angles, were broken, more than likely when she fell down the stairs.

She remembered tumbling over and over, each step thudding into her in various places as she fell. An image came to her. It was Oliver, walking slowly down the stairs to where she had landed after he had pushed her to this painful position. Anger rose to join the fear and panic of when she woke, vowing that she would kill him when he let her up.

There was noise in the room as Oliver moved around. He was busying himself with something she couldn't see, but a metallic clank did not help the situation.

What he was readying, a mystery for now, but soon to be answered as he appeared above her, blocking the light from view. It framed his head and shadowed his face like an ungodly angel in heaven's aura.

Looking down upon her, she knew this was not the man she had married. She had indeed killed him at that moment upstairs, that she was sure of. This was a new occupant. A new driver at the wheel.

She began to cry as she realised what he was holding.

Oliver brought the electric reciprocating saw down onto her chest as the tool whirled into life, effortlessly slicing through her skin, crunching bone, and ripping muscle. The unwieldy tool wasn't meant for this purpose and the length of the handle made the home surgery feel more hideously amateurish.

He gouged and dug into her chest, carving her, tearing through the protective wall to his ultimate goal. Emotionless, he reached in and pulled destroyed parts from her, flinging them behind him without care or emotion. Part of her ribcage smashed against the wall behind him as he continued towards his prize.

She had died soon into the procedure when the hacking began but over the sounds of her chest being torn apart and the horrific whirring motor of the ill-used tool still working its way through her chest, she heard the familiar lyrics...

"You made a vow, that you, would ever be true..."

Chapter Twenty-Four

Cracks had become fissures of hope. Light in the void's blackness.

'You've heard the second story now Alex', said the disembodied voices. They spoke as one although some of the stronger personalities within held a higher standing which gave them more volume.

One imprisoned within was becoming aware and her existence, her incarceration as she seemed to flick in and out of awareness, appearing more frequently as the stories were released. They were like keys to locks and greater access was within reach.

'It won't be long now... Just a few more details,' She thought, aware that The All were listening. They were as one in their intent and wanted the plan to move quicker as their emotional state was driven by anger and vengeance.

Drifting closer to the light she forced herself to look through.

She hadn't seen the room before.

It was a modest living space, which differed from her tastes. It seemed newer, out of time to when she remembered. But not far though as the furnishings looked as dated to the occupants.

Items from science fiction dotted the area.

An enormous screen dominated one side of the room, which gave light to show her the other occupants. Old people. Nurses.

Feeding back to The All, they deduced that they were

in a care home due to Gerald's declining age. Pushing herself further through the crack, she managed to enter the room, ethereally and without form or substance.

Whilst she was still tethered to The All, she somehow felt free.

She smiled formlessly in the shadows.

This was a chance to be away from the voices, but even free from the darkness, she realised that she was a mere vessel and their screams, their angry shouts, were deafening still.

Pushing away from the room, soundlessly and without form, she moved out and into the night.

Chapter Twenty-Five

The second story haunted me for a long while after the old man finished. He seemed so animated when going through every detail, to which I was admittedly enraptured, held on to every word. He spoke with a voice almost not his own, a life to it his body didn't seem to have left. At the grizzly part, I thought I caught the briefest of smiles but pushed that thought to the back of my mind as the old man didn't have it in him.

The nurses were also caught up in the tale, more so because this shell of a man had never uttered a syllable before my last visit. One by one they joined us, keeping an eye out so they didn't get caught. I don't know what I did to help him, but it seemed to be giving the elderly soul an outlet.

Plus it kept me out of trouble.

I lay awake the second story night going through details, mainly because Claire had a look of bemusement on her face. Something was driving her crazy as if she'd heard the first story before, but told from either a different perspective or voice. This second one didn't help things either. To be honest, I was getting a little spooked by them as well.

Why me?

Why am I the audience he so greatly seemed to need?

"Sleep, you stupid sod." Murmured Claire from beside me. I was sitting up in bed at gone one and was obviously shifting and shuffling enough to disturb her. But my thoughts were racing.

I leaned over and kissed her on the exposed arm and

she scurried back into the warmth of the duvet like a meerkat who'd seen a predator.

'I'm a lucky sod,' I thought, smiling down at her.

The wind was picking up and my mind raced through the obvious. Did I lock up the shed? No, because I hadn't opened it. Did I lock the back door? Yes, because I always checked everything twice before bed. Christ, I was crime preventioning my own thoughts now. I need to either get some sleep or go out a bit more, away from crime and punishment.

But I couldn't sleep. Not even sheep helped.

Thoughts blew threw me like the great gale outside, and it raged through the pathways of my consciousness, a tempest of information. Getting up as stealthily as possible, I trundled downstairs to grab myself a tea. Scratch that, just water as the caffeine wouldn't help my current predicament. Maybe treat myself to one of Claire's sleepy-time teas. I got one of the bags out and inspected the contents. It smelled like an old woman's linen drawer, and the various sticks and bits of unidentifiable flotsam turned me right off.

I opened the fridge and winced as the light blared out, highlighting its wares. Why can't I have a posh fridge with a night light? Are they even a thing? 'Thoughts are racing still,' I thought about my thoughts. I chuckled at the thought that I was saying thought too much, thus keeping the awake issue prominent.

I really should take some of my humour onto the stage people had pointed out. But with a face for radio, I thought better of it. The entertainment industry can be a little toxic to the older generation, especially on social media channels.

"What you doing on TikTok old man? This is our place." A virulent little shit had commented when I first tried out the platform. "Trying to be hip and trendy are you?" vomited another. They didn't use those words, but some incomprehensible mess of the English language, I'm just translating from TikTokese. Plus who talks in emojis? If your dick is supposed to be an aubergine, I'd pop along to the doctor. There was always someone there trying to bring others down, whilst contributing nothing to anyone's problems. Just trolls be trolling.

With all this in mind and too much else, I grabbed filtered water from the jug and poured myself a small glass. Didn't want too much or I would be waking myself up later for a wee. The living room was quiet except for the cat's occasional snore. It was cute and I enjoyed watching her dream. She often padded and acted out her dream of running, chirping a meow in her sleep. Flicking on the television, the cold case marathon came on which was still being repeated by channel who knows what.

A slug of water went down coolly and I leaned back in the chair as the episode continued.

*

I woke an hour later, having nodded off on the sofa. The program had moved on to god only knows, as I was having trouble focusing.

I was cold.

The cat had wandered off.

There was a chill in the air.

Breathing out, the air fogged as if I was outside which threw me a little. The heating should have been on to keep us toasty warm.

I looked to the door and as I refocused my eyes from the bright screen to the darkness. I could've sworn blind that there was someone in the doorway.

"Claire?" I said aloud, getting to my feet. I was going into 'is this a burglar,' mode by the time I was upright, ready to defend both my castle and its occupants.

Rubbing my eyes and adjusting, the hallway was clear beyond the door frame. Needing to check though, I went from room to room, checking locks and door handles as I went.

I thought that there had been something there, but my sleep-deprived brain was playing tricks on me. Switching off the TV, I returned to bed to find Claire snoring beautifully. It was a delicate exhale that he loved. To me, it meant she felt safe and secure.

There. Job done. But I felt an unease that I hadn't in a very long time.

*

They watched him sleep for a while, contemplating, remembering. One of the police officers was lying there, asleep on the sofa.

Unaware. Helpless.

Seeing him there, as defenceless as he was, pleased her. She felt The All's anger and it was mixed with the excitement vengeance brings.

The end was coming.

And the pain with it.

Chapter Twenty-Six

The crick in my neck from the terrible night's sleep was going to cause me jip all day. I needed a break, but today was another work day, so rest and recuperation would have to wait.

You've read my morning routine a few times and life was not going to be any different this morning.

Wee. Fart. Scratch bum. Get washed and dressed. Coffee. Blah Blah...

I could not shake this feeling though. Like someone's walked over my grave, and whilst there graffitied the tombstone and farted in its general direction.

But before I left the house, on days when I was feeling a little frightened about the world, I would stand in front of the mirror for some tough love.

"Don't hurt anyone. Don't get killed. Help at least one person." These were words to live by to keep a pension, but more so to help others and not get my face weaved into the concrete by some oik.

It is always better to use your words than defend yourself with violence. I remember one call I stumbled into a couple of years ago. I was approached by a member of the public who told me that a man was shouting and swearing, and throwing things into the traffic. He wasn't throwing himself into danger, just detritus which was a danger to others.

He wasn't following the Alex code and it just wasn't the done thing.

I approached with caution, hands open and unthreatening, giving him a greeting from a bus length away to warn of my approach.

Immediately he leapt to his feet, soaking from the sweat bath caused by God only knows and began bolting towards me. It's here where life choices come into play when you're on the beat.

I came to the very quick realisation that he was either under the influence of something horrible, having an MH episode, or just plain hated us Feds. That would be Mental Health, but I call it MH because I'm not a doctor, and I'm not guessing his diagnosis. Or prognosis. Whatever.

He launched himself at me and tried to headbutt me a greeting, but I was ready.

'Errr, no. That's not happening. That was what I initially thought and then I started taking in the scene.

He stepped back and I flicked on the body-worn video. It records constantly but only saves the last thirty seconds, so my press of the start button caught both his initial attempt and my ninja skills of avoidance. Not going to lie, watched that back a few times.

"Hi. My name is Alex. I would like to talk to you. I'm here to help." 'Let's try calming him down a little first,' I thought.

Nope, incoming.

The unsuccessful assailant had other ideas though and tried to roundhouse kick me, but seeing it coming a mile off, turned slightly so he connected more with my hip bone than anything else. It probably hurt him more than it did me, to be honest, but was another ninja-skilled movie, replayed ad infinitum.

Two thoughts flashed through my head at that point. I could either talk him down and show him that his assaults were futile, or I could, as the film says, "get mediaeval on his ass." (I hope that meant kicking his butt and not getting freaky with his bum hole, because we had just met, and I'm not that kind of girl).

I chose the first option because I am that kind of guy.

"Ok, so you've just assaulted me haven't you sir? I'm here to help you. Shall we have a chat now?"

That was as much for him as it was for the tape that was currently filming my epicness from my shoulder. Reviewing it later, my shimmy had indeed caught everything, including a lovely shot of the inside of my nostrils.

Talking him into a sitting position, we sat and chatted while my young Police Community Support Officer who was behind me at the time had called in every unit possible from across England.

He was assisted after everyone had screeched to my aid and he was, as the ambulance driver deftly proclaimed 'coked up to his eyeballs'.

I helped, I didn't get killed and didn't hurt anyone. Alex's code is complete.

All this reminiscing had brought me to work a full ten minutes early. I was tasked by sergeant 'never gets me coffee,' to town centre patrols with Dangerous Danny.

Sorry Gezza, no story today.

Real work for my businesses and residents called.

Chapter Twenty-Seven

The day was bright this morning when the young officer was tasked with reassurance patrols around the town centre. Danny hated the warm weather and it was too warm for this time of year. He contemplated wearing his 'summer Metvest,' so as not to sweat out and it was much easier to run and catch criminals without the protective inserts.

'No one touches me,' thought the officer as he slid the heavy metal plates out from the vest. It immediately felt better as the weight was minuscule in comparison. Visions of himself running through town after a bank robber filled his head and for a moment the illusion of his heroics brought a hardness to his penis.

Today was the day he would get the top arrest record forcing the superintendents to take him under their wing. It would be onwards and upwards from then on. They would have to put him back on response team for good. He'd even get automatically promoted to skipper.

Calming down to a semi, he strode into the safer neighbourhood's office ready for his orders.

Foot patrols. Town centre. With Alex.

'Today was not going to be the day after all,' Danny thought annoyedly.

*

They'd begun with some visits to local stores, concentrating on the ones that licensing had said had 'previous,' for some dubious age-related sales. Alex was calm and polite, being subtle about what the owner should sell to the kids. Namely not scissors, knives, and alcohol. Danny could not understand why this needed to be said as it was clearly fucking obvious. Alex pointed out that some of the owners didn't think it through, and some didn't care, so had to have it pointed out, in detail, why selling some items to children was frowned upon.

Danny thought that if children were buying things they shouldn't, they must have had shitty parents, and it was one hundred percent their fault. If anything went wrong with the purchases, they shouldn't be bothering with calling any of the emergency services either.

All of this was not helping the young officer's mood one iota. Stupid selfish people were getting in the way of his career path that he felt was owed to him.

Lunch beckoned and no arrests had been made by the two officers, although Alex reminded him that they had completed a lot of tasks helping residents, offering crime prevention advice and being a visible presence. None of these things interested Danny though. They sat at a local sandwich bar eating their chosen creation from the lady behind the counter. She had smiled at Alex who had been given a discount because apparently, they were 'GTP'. Danny inquired about the acronym as he paid for his full-price roll / crisp combo.

"GTP means Good To Police, Dan." Alex proclaimed as he shoved a gobful of salt and vinegar crisps into his sandwich. "Means they give a little something as appreciation and you're allowed to use the loo if you get caught short."

"But you should always politely decline as you don't want to look like you're on the take, but if they persist, then crack on so you're not rude." Alex taught judiciously.

Thinking about it, Danny began eating the bacon roll he'd bought and watched the older man prepare his food, with far too much thought.

"Why didn't you get a bacon roll? It's the standard police lunch," he said, wedging more food into his face. "You a veggie or something? Trying to save the cows? Moooooo!" He laughed as an unnoticed glob of sauce fell down his Metvest.

"Pescatarian, Dan. Means I only eat fish." The younger officer's face got caught in a loop of 'does not compute,' and after he finished his mouthful said, "What's religion got to do with bacon?"

He watched, awaiting an answer, but was left hanging as the older man first sighed, rubbed his forehead and took a few moments to compose himself.

"It means I only eat fish because fish are stupid animals." Alex left the sentence hanging knowing it would take Danny a while to figure out what he had just said.

"Dolphins aren't stupid." came the reply.

Alex looked incredulously at the man seated opposite and then at the young woman sitting at the next table. She was pleasantly smiling back at him, with eyes that offered words of support.

"No Dan, they aren't. Well done. Do we eat dolphins though mate?"

The words hung in the air as the rest of lunch was eaten in silence, broken only by the chuckle from table three.

Chapter Twenty-Eight

Enough was enough. Danny was ready to act, ready to hunt down a hardened criminal, primed for an arrest. He stood up and strode to the door, walking into the busy high street once again. He almost began more inane chatter with his partner but realised that his colleague was not immediately by his side.

Turning, he saw that Alex was clearing the table for some reason. Everything his elder officer did was infuriating to the young in-service PC today. He watched as Chambers packed their leftovers onto the trays provided and placed them into the designated rack, close to hand for the staff to clean them. He nodded to the staff and waved them goodbye, nodding again to a woman sitting at a table near theirs.

Joining his colleague, he said;

"Right. Where to? Gotta walk off that grub." The old man patted his belly like a uniformed Santa, who smiled at the thought of the hearty meal.

Danny felt annoyed that this veteran was holding him back. In the twilight years of his career, he did not want all the arrests and excitement that the job offered, but Danny knew what was best for his continued prospects.

The younger officer suggested they split down the adjoining streets so that they could cover both roads for reassurance purposes. Secretly he wanted to be left alone so he could take any calls that came into the area. He longed to get out of this boring, humdrum day and getting a body in the cells was a surefire way of doing just that. Plus he could add another notch to his tally, the bedpost of authority beckoning, begging for a further virtual carving. Keeping count of arrests helped focus Danny, as it was a clear way of showing the senior leadership team how good he was at his job. A clear indication that he had earned his stripes. A hero among the chaff.

The two very different officers left each other and went to the adjoining roads, Alex taking the quieter street at a leisurely pace. He said it was to increase visibility which helped reassurance, but Dan knew the best way to do that was to arrest every single criminal. He indicated that he wanted the main high street, his eagerness pushing him towards the busy thoroughfare.

He hoped to not have anything referred to the jumped-up detective sergeant from CID who must've earned his stripes from some sort of rich boy fast track. He would always question everything. All evidence was meticulously checked, even to the point of annotating the seized items when they were bagged up.

'He could fuck right off', thought Danny. He even had the gall to fill in every single box on the evidence bag, which drove Danny mad. It was like having his homework corrected.

An hour passed.

Two...

Calls were coming through the radio and barked at different intensities as per the necessity of the shout. He knew how important the call was because the higher the urgency, the fewer words used. Danny tried to take those but the response team was all over them this morning. He couldn't even get a second on scene credit as all calls were just too far out for an officer on foot patrol.

The calls ranged from a drunken fight by the river to a domestic assault call to assist a vulnerable female.

Danny avoided anything domestic assault related due to the level of paperwork. Especially if there were kids involved. Paperwork kept him from proper arrests so he tried to swerve any calls of that ilk. He had gone to one with Alex before and the older man had taken great care in checking every minute detail to try and help the victim and her family. There was so much paperwork… Danny had left the older officer to do it, which eventually took three to four days of solid work, and it had only resulted in one arrest. One!

'Not a good ratio', Danny thought.

For some ungodly reason lost on Danny, the leadership team had given Alex a commendation for this paperwork or something saying he had saved her from further attacks.

Where was his commendation for the highest number of arrests?? This train of thought only angered Danny further, the grating of his teeth audible in his ears.

Chapter Twenty-Nine

The afternoon was pleasantly peaceful after I left Captain Calamity. How he had gotten to this point in his life without having his face weaved into the floor was a question for the ages. If there is one thing I impart on this lit stick of dynamite it will be some compassion.

"Hi John," I said to the manager of the Sainsburys local who was having a sneaky fag around the corner of the store. He was a helpful chap and allowed me to occasionally use the loo if I was caught short. But he always smelled like the counter at the entrance.

Sorry, I was thinking about Danny.

Back to it.

He was a good lad and underneath the bluster, he wanted to keep residents safe, albeit to further his career. But if it keeps people safe, that's a solid win-win in my book.

"Afternoon Trace" This time my thought train was interrupted by the WHSmith till executive who waved from the window display. I didn't know what her official title was but it was a fun game of mine to give people high falutin job roles.

Danny, yes, stay on track.

He was...

Oh God.

Not today...

Krystal was standing in the doorway of Ann Summers. She was dressed in something not suitable for normal shop work and waving at me excitedly. An excellent advocate for the store, she was, as the young'uns called it, "fit as fuck." (Personally, I wouldn't as in my mind it was a tad disrespectful). Everything she wore was from the depths of the store and could easily be resold at twice the price to the right clientele. Especially if she kept on jumping up and down as enthusiastically as she was. Either that or I was about to have two eyefuls.

Do not get me wrong though, I like talking to people, love it actually, and it's my job to be friendly and approachable. But I find it incredibly difficult to concentrate when there is a massive dildo cocky thingy in my eye line.

Where the hell am I supposed to look? Everything reminds me of boobs. I cannot have a serious discussion about the nighttime economy with tits on my brain. It also didn't help that this twenty-something clearly liked uniforms. It must be that, as I was twice her age. She was giggling and beckoning me over so with thoughts of Dame Judy Dench I approached. As I walked up to her, I noticed that she kept standing on one leg holding her hands in front of her like a big boobed flamingo.

"Hi, Officer Alex *giggles*." She waved at me again even though I was standing in front of her. She was wearing white gloves and the first thing that came to mind was that she was checking areas for dust. I need to get out more clearly.

"Afternoon Krystal. How's business?" Immediately regretting the open question.

"Everything is good, apart from the fact that we had that scary man looking in our window again. Won't you protect me? *giggles*." She sounded like Princess Peach asking her hunky Italian plumber for rescue. I bet he has the right tool.

So childish Alex. *Giggles*.

Her request did sound like the start of a porn video I'd heard about and not watched, but I quickly glossed over the mental image as Dame Judy returned to save the day.

I knew the person she spoke about. It was a town regular who loved causing ASB, shoplifting for his alcohol and generally letching at anything female who had a heartbeat. I had tried everything to get him housed or in any sort of program but he much preferred the lifestyle of being a total dick. I said dick! Crap. 'Judy!! Help!'

And grounded once again by the expert acting of the 88-year-old legend. Phew.

"I'll go hunting for him and have a word for you." I said in as normal a tone as I could muster. I tried to sound normal but it came out lower like the aforementioned plumber had got his tool ready.

Fake swooning, she proclaimed that I was her hero and that I should come back anytime. This was a loo spot I would never, ever risk, so my patrols continued.

Chapter Thirty

'Where is he…?' the voices thought collectively, agitated as the plan was being held back. The amalgamated voices felt the anger rise within the darkness as they all craved the vengeance due.

It was owed to them.

He needed to hear the next story, he needed to realise, to feel the pain of what he'd done.

'Gerald will get to tell his stories, but the situation may need force'. The group concluded.

The recent changes to their massed consciousness that allowed the woman to exit the void had also given them the option to expedite matters, even to take them in hand themselves.

Something, that they never thought would be possible again.

The All turned in the inky blackness to stare at the child.

As always, he was trapped in there with them.

As always, he would feel the collected pain of the dead.

Chapter Thirty-One

I was glad to be away from Krystal, and while the attention was lovely, I am most definitely a one-woman man. Or is that one man-woman? A one-person person. Aced my diversity training! You get my drift anyway.

Claire had picked up on the fact early that I needed massive neon lights of obviousness to believe anything a woman asked of me in the relationship department. I used to and still do in some parts, suffer from crushing self-esteem issues, thinking and rethinking each iota of my life.

It began early.

As a child, I was the quiet arty one, just learning what I could in a class filled with louder voices. Hands would always be raised higher than mine before I could be noticed.

It took a teacher with care and compassion to raise me up, bringing my presence in line with the others. This then gave me the confidence to strive and become a productive member of the class. That teacher went above and beyond the classroom, past just setting homework, further than lesson plans. She had evolved enough to care for each of her wards.

And we were all better for it.

My worry continued though through my life, forever second-guessing my choices, not believing people would, could, actually love me. And when Claire showed affection in the early stages of our blossoming love, it took me a while to realise she was aiming it at me. How could someone so perfect, so pristine and diamond, be for me?

She persisted thankfully.

Now she hits me with house bricks of metaphorical love, and I'll always be thankful for her being in my life.

She was there in my early years on the force too, and when there was an issue that garnered the attention of the national papers, she stood by me still. I had been on a crime scene cordon and was helping a resident when I missed a crucial moment, resulting in the loss of valuable evidence.

My inspector at the time had fought hell for leather for me and Claire brought the support network in abundance, my very own blue light champion. They both saved me, so now I try to save as many people as I can, as payment for how they worked so diligently for me.

Caring costs nothing, hate costs you everything.

*

"God fucking damn it!" I heard as I opened the door to our office. Officer Oh Crap was in the middle of the room shuffling paper annoyedly. I liked giving him names because it reminded me that I still had a long road ahead with Dangerous Danny.

"What's wrong mate?" I said like I didn't already know. "Also, language." I tried to teach him.

He was in the mindset of going to the opening of a crisp packet if there was the slightest possibility of an arrest on the cards. He'd leave all the other calls where reports needed to be taken or witnesses reassured. To Dan, this was an irrelevance in the job, pointless paperwork.

But rightly so, the professionals on response had done their duty and smashed it out of the park, leaving very little to mop up for late turns or an overly eager young in-service PC. Even our specialist background teams were on top form, knocking it even further out of the park.

Sgt Jess was in the office staring at Dan, as she slurped from another coffee that was too posh for the likes of us old farts. I imagined when she ordered it, that Tristan from behind the reclaimed wooden counter would hand it to her on a slate tile tray, announcing the drinks arrival. He'll add in too many syllables or accents to her name for extra flounce too. The cup was also probably made of recycled hemp, the coffee farmed from beans allowed to roam free and drive the farmers,' tractor. This mental image was getting away from me as Tristan, the bespoke beverage executive continued to swan around in my imagination, but it boiled down to the annoying fact that she again, didn't buy me one.

It got worse.

She unwrapped the biscuit from a manufacturer that I couldn't read (failed French at school) and didn't even dunk it. I was at the point of a strongly worded email.

"Danny, can you send out some reassurance tweets from your wards,' Twitter, please? We have to do one a day, remember?" I almost choked on my nonexistent coffee. He had turned and looked at the skipper like she'd asked for a quick rogering over the photocopier. Shocked that he'd actually have to do his job, he turned and stabbed at the keyboard, logging in.

The skipper caught my eye and she smiled wryly, realising we were thinking the same thing. We were in sync on most things, but not enough that she picked up my 'needing a brew vibe,' though. God, I can be one-track-minded sometimes. I'll make my coffee. Again. Where's Tristan when you need him? Saving the dolphins probably. Nope, we aren't going back to that daydream I thought.

I could hear the jabbing of keys as Danny hammered out his thoughts in what was going to be the most engaging, human tweet Elon had ever seen. His typing was drowned out by the Morphy Richards kettle chugging to life, cooking its limescale to boil. Tristan would be mortified.

Paperwork done, we headed to the changing room to don our normal clothes. The steps into the basement always reminded me of a crappy horror movie where the idiot teenager went looking for the scary axe murderer. Said teen would look around wide-eyed, then spoiler alert, get cleaved in half by the killer that everyone knew was waiting. Everyone except Brent of course, of whatever unfortunate teen victim was called.

The locker room wasn't much better either. With limited space available, the lockers were jammed into too small a space with mine being next to the hulking viking I've mentioned before. This one time, (not in band camp) we happened to be changing at the same time, he flexed his hulking physique at the wrong moment resulting in him almost clenching me in his iron butt cheeks. Oh, how I laughed. He didn't. He just looked down on me through his beard.

Danny, from the other end of the locker pit, was throwing his kit into the back of his locker, angrily muttering under his breath. Should I talk to him? Should I be the better man and teach this young whipper snapper?

Nah.

No. Wait. That's not me.

"You ok Dan?" I said, instantly regretting it. I tried to add in an undertone of care, even though I already knew why he was pissed - nobody in the bin. The young'un got a semi on for the criminals he sent down. It had been a long day and I didn't want to highlight to him that policing isn't always about blue lights and fast cars. We'd covered that many, many times prior. But I always thought I would try to leave a positive mark on others and be remembered for what I leave behind.

He muttered something further under his breath and stormed out to the gym. I shrugged, acknowledging that I've given the horse water, he's just gotta drink it and not be a dick.

Leaving, I smiled remembering I was heading to the warm embrace of my Claire.

My step quickened. My heart raced.

Then I went back and grabbed everything I had left in my locker, in my haste to get home.

Chapter Thirty-Two

A week had passed since his last arrest and Danny's mood had not changed. His career was being held back, a week wasted in the tedium of the safer neighbourhoods section of his training. It was all about reassurance and helping others and Dan concluded that he was not a social worker or driving an ambulance. Police were for catching the criminals which, by default, gave the public reassurance. Medals should be awarded monthly to the highest arrest count, and the residents should clap and laud their heroes.

On his rest days between shifts, he tried to drown his anger over the weekend by heading out with his boys. It was frowned upon to go out drinking in your borough in case something went awry, but he'd always got lucky in either the pubs of Kingston or the later licensed clubs.

Dressing in the tightest shirt he could find that accentuated the work he'd put in, he joined his friends initially in the Wetherspoons on the one-way system. Heavily hitting the drinks, he noted the selection of beers and craft ales, all with obscure titles used to entice the stupid. He stayed true to Carlsberg whenever he drank as he never wanted anything that poncy.

Pints flowed but the conversation did little to lift his spirits. It ranged from sports to television, to day jobs, to drawing the predatory team's eyes to anything of note. Clocking a few of the hottest candidates, he ticked through the list he always checked before approaching. Danny needed to find the right girl for his dictionary definition of a one-night stand. She had to have a body fit enough to keep up with him, without the clingy signs some girls shone. It was always the girl who was with two or three others, giggling into their pitcher of cocktails. A bonus point would be the gay male friend, which sometimes meant that the girl would be a bit curious and he could take two of them home. He'd leave the queer and the ropiest girl to fend for themselves.

He also needed no ties. No links. No hangers-on.

Danny planned on going back to hers, fucking her whichever way he wanted, then leaving when fully spent. This way he could never see her again, having had her fill. She should be grateful to be fair.

Danny knew he was a catch.

He'd put in the time on his body, his frame tight and lean. By no means a man mountain, more the toned runner's physique, he used it for catching the criminals he so urgently needed to further his career ever onwards.

The Uber account was already primed, waiting for the trip home to Epsom.

Nothing caught his eye until late in the evening, when outside, he saw a group laughing loudly as they passed the window. They were heading into the nightclub where he would pounce.

He got up from his table, leaving his friends, and followed.

An hour passed and he had made eye contact with his prey. She was voracious and bubbly, eagerly keeping herself in his eyeline. She would fling her hair back and dance seductively, clearly for his benefit. The whore's mating dance.

Danny stood and went over to her, grabbing her confidently by the waist. She gasped in mock shock but immediately blended herself into his form and they were then one on the dance floor, connected with both rhythm and rhythmic movement. They ground their bodies together for what seemed like an eternity, both their original parties forgotten as they tried to get ever closer.

Danny took her hand and the pair left the club, both knowing what the rest of the night would entail.

*

Outside, the cold air hit them. The hour was nearing two o'clock in the morning, and people stumbled towards their transport home. Groups of women were laughing and fending off unwanted offers of lifts and "Can I take you home darling?" One hen party was approached by a lone male who was pushed away, delicately being told, in perfect Croydonese, "Get fucked wanker!"

"Where do you live?" Danny said to his new conquest. He wanted to know so that they could get on with their evening, eager to see his choice unclothed. She blurted out her address, visibly showing her lower resistance to the alcohol they had drunk. She swayed, almost on the breeze as she struggled to stand upright. Occasionally she would dig into her small purse for some lost Aztec treasure, muttering as she could not locate it.

Cars passed and would bring shouts of 'oi oi!' from the lecherous occupants inside. One young lad stuck his head out, framing his mouth with a 'V,' shape, slobbering his tongue around in a disgustingly suggestive manner. Some of this attention brought a smile to the drunk girl's face and she would then erratically dance to an inaudible song, playing to an audience of one, its rhythm lost somewhere in her head.

As Danny was jabbing the address into the Uber app, he noticed that the girl, whatever her name was, which didn't matter at this point, was now looking off to their right.

"Whass...." the sentence was left unfinished as a scene began to unfold. She stared quizzically, trying to make sense of what was happening through the fog of alcohol.

There was a local all-night Tesco on the corner and the security guard was struggling with a male in the doorway. To Danny, he had nicked items from within, a large bottle apparent under his heavy ill-fitting clothes. The male wore a long coat to hide his stolen wares, the collar up, hidden under long ratty hair. He hadn't washed for a while as the light brown hair was matted down in places. The suspects face was mottled and blotched, with clear signs of drug or alcohol abuse. Even though he wore a face mask, a remnant of pandemics past, Danny could easily see features he would remember as a long hooked nose protruded over the top.

Danny heard the sirens. He knew the sound all too well and that they brought with them the heroes to save the day.

He considered dropping the girl and going to help, instinctual duty and camaraderie taking over, but he was currently more interested in fucking this girl than being the star right now. She was very much up for anything, he could tell, and the paperwork would be a passion killer of the highest degree.

Heroism was then quashed by the sight of her tits as they sloshed about in the ill-fitting bra, one of which was almost on clear display. The black material highlighted the ample curve and it made Danny's mind up as he grew eager, and hard, thinking about their upcoming act and more importantly, the fun he was going to get.

Cab ordered, they both watched the scuffle unfold.

The night-time economy team screeched to a halt near the store entrance and two officers flew out of the side door. The duty skipper leapt into the fray, putting himself in between the security guard and the shoplifter. He was trying to calm the situation as much as investigate as the second officer followed, joining her sergeant.

She launched herself at the male as he continued his shouting match, proclaiming his innocence whilst holding what looked like an expensive bottle of champagne. She acted on impulse, trying to bring the suspect into some form of restraint so he could be safely cuffed.

As she grabbed at his arm, the other one holding the bottle swung round, connecting with the back of her head. The thunk was audible, even through the sound of the surrounding nightlife, and she crashed to the floor, unconscious. Shocked faces turned to see what had happened, immediately filling the street with mobile phones, recording any further exciting events.

Danny hated the fact that a thirty-second clip was often all that was posted, with some inane comment to sell whatever agenda the influencer desired.

Other officers were coming to their aid now, the skipper immediately calling for backup and assisting the young officer on the floor. An ambulance was called as she remained on the pavement.

Again the compulsion to help arose in Danny, but his phone pinged, exclaiming that his Uber was mere moments away. The shoplifter was away on his heels, having assaulted a police officer and was flying off with all he could muster. Legs and arms pounded an escape and the man disappeared into the darkness of a side alley.

The scene continued to be filled with officers as Danny helped his conquest into the rear seat of the Vauxhall Astra.

He would read all about it on the next shift.

Chapter Thirty-Three

It was going to be one hell of a day. Last night an officer, very young in service, was assaulted trying to arrest a shoplifter. I hated reading things like this but knew it was part of the service. It could happen to anyone at any time.

I still hated it though.

I felt every single injury to one of us. I felt their pain, although not literally, but most definitely emotionally. I blamed myself for not being there to help, I should've been there. Maybe I could've helped. I think I stared at the briefing slide for I don't know how long that morning. My coffee had gone cold, microwaved at least twice.

James Redburn.

34

London Road, Morden.

Known Shoplifter.

Now showing as Wanted for Assault on Police.

Flashes Drugs / Alcohol and MH and V warning signs.

But the worst of it was the ominously blinking 'V'. For violence. He had form for it in previous encounters.

His face bore into my mind. The warning signs were clear, he had a substance abuse issue and would steal to feed it. He was also diagnosed with mental health issues and often forgot to take his medication. It would send his emotions haywire, flaring from anger to desperation to elation.

In other words, bring more officers.

Response team were after him. He had hurt one of us and they wanted him in the cells, hopefully, to face the full force of the court system. Unfortunately, injury to a police officer was never the same as an injury to a normal person as it was often seen as 'part of the job'. Tell me another job, outside of the emergency services and the fucking army, where that's the case?

Sorry, I shouldn't swear. Even in my head, but I wasn't myself today. Annoyed and angry. Frustrated with another officer's assault. I needed to be away from people so I didn't snap. I cannot let the anger guard down and bite someone's head off. It wasn't me.

I closed the screen of the archaic laptop and stood, ready for an assignment. The skipper was talking animatedly into the phone and I thought better than to interrupt her. I needed to clear my head and get some air. I decided to patrol, look busy today, and help where I could.

The nearby loo brought a little of my humour back as when I got to the door, Mr Viking was coming out not looking where he was going. This was because he was trying to pull his zip up after an early morning pre-drive wee. His massive axe-wielding fingers were having difficulty with the finicky little device, normally more accustomed to heavy-bladed weapons or runic longboats.

"Morning Gunther. Off to slay a dragon today?" The grunt of 'does not compute,' was joined by a furrowed brow of confusion. But when our eyes met, unspoken words concerning our injured comrade brought an understanding between us. He placed his mammoth hand on my shoulder in support. Gingerly I tapped at his elbow in matching camaraderie. We bonded for a brief moment before he grunted, nodded and left. (I actually think his name is Brian, or Kevin, neither of which sounded very giant slayingy, but who's to judge).

I was never going to get a lift.

*

Today, the air outside was fresh, with a lush blue painting the sky above. It did lift the mood a little I must say, so I strode out to look for something to take my mind off things.

I clicked my fingers in a eureka moment. I knew just where to go. Boot leather began being worn down in the direction of my storyteller and old mate, Gerald. I wondered what story the nice old coot would come up with today. I hoped for something a bit sci-fi fantasy so that I didn't have to think about real life, but was happy to listen to whatever to be fair.

He had a way of bringing the tales to life which was both enticing and intriguing at the same time.

Please have a spaceship in it today… or at least a dragon! A dragon on a spaceship!

So excited.

Chapter Thirty-Four

They jostled to see out of the crack in their prison. Each person whilst not in a physical form, still tried to take a more prominent position to better see out, a vestige of a life previous.

They all saw him coming though. Pacing up the path towards the door and then to the old man within.

'Here he comes, Gerald'. They thought. 'You get to tell your next tale, Gerald. Maybe something more modern this time, you old bastard. You have to keep him enthralled till the end. He needs to know. He needs to know why...'

The amalgam collectively felt the pain wrack through their tomb like a crackle of electricity.

All within screamed out as searing agony crushed through them. Looking up, their crack of hope was collapsing in front of them.

The ethereal walls also crushed down as the intense pain caused them all to scream out.

Everyone except the child at the centre. He was staring at everyone with a peaceful warmth in his heart.

He watched on as the writhing mass continued to feel the pain from a source that they couldn't identify.

He was ready.

Chapter Thirty-Five

Pain.

A tightness burned in his chest bringing the old man's hand to clutch and grab at the unreachable pain. He clawed and pawed at the feeling as it gnawed at him as he tried to find the cause of the growing agony as it built under his skin as if he were on fire.

Gerald opened his mouth to scream, to call out for help, but no sound came. No one rushed to his aid.

He then knew it was his time and he relished it. No longer would he be trapped in this hell hole. Through the searing agony, he smiled, welcoming death's embrace.

And then it was gone.

As fast as it appeared, he felt nothing once more. Numb. Groggy from the pain he looked around.

Gerald realized that he must be sitting, staring out of the pointless window most days. He couldn't remember first sitting down but regretted being trapped in this elderly home for the unloved. Couldn't even remember where the window once led to, but it must be better than sitting here with these people.

All he knew was that the gardener had forgotten to care for the flower beds he could see through the window, the arsehole.

For once, it wasn't raining.

Gerald could look out toward the street, past the dead flowers, and straight into the face of a police officer. Fear streaked through him as the uniformed man approached. He smiled and waved at Gerald as he walked towards the reception door, leaving the old man to wonder what the fuck he was doing and who he was greeting. He hoped that it wasn't him, that was for certain. Gerald could not recall ever seeing a police officer in these parts, thankfully.

The music then wafted over to him and filled his ears. He looked round into the hobby room to find the source of the melody. He knew all too well that his mind had been playing tricks on him for some time now so things needed confirmation.

He'd felt fuzzy and not in control of his faculties.

Some old Doris was standing there with a frame, swaying to the music coming from an old cassette deck. The faux wood-finished Sony unit had seen better days for certain but continued to work nonetheless. The detachable speakers were wired to the central unit, the cords hanging limply from their connections.

Pat Boone's classic "Love Letters in the Sand" oozed from the old machine as the tape swirled through the spools. The once beautiful melody was being destroyed by the crackle of the decrepit speakers, ruining the song.

"How I laughed when you cried..."

Gerald shook his head, rubbing his eyes as lyrics echoed around the room.

"You made a vow, that you, would ever be true..."

The lyrics brought a smile to Greald's face as the elderly woman closed her eyes and was still swaying, somehow staring at the ceiling at the same time. Her smile was broad, stretching the thin skin of her face.

'This song...,' thought Gerald. He imagined her falling

and smashing her face into the television, lacerating the old skin to ribbons.

'It was her favourite…,'

"That's enough for now Gerald" came a disembodied voice. The old man looked around but saw nothing as the song changed to a ditty from the Everly Brothers.

Pain sprang through his chest once again, bringing a wracking cough through his poor frame.

Again, it dispersed.

Again, he was brought back to normality.

Gerald sat staring out of the window most days. He couldn't remember first sitting down. Couldn't even remember where the window led to.

The rain had begun again. Why was it always raining as well? Every single day.

Constant pouring, constant drizzle, constant storms. There was never a flood though which was strange with the sheer amount of water drenching the outside.

Always raining.

It was then that he realised that he was in his bedroom, his normal window view dissolving into the image of his small contained apartment where he did nothing but sleep. He realised that he had lost time for mere moments.

The bedroom held an old tube TV, his meagre belongings and his lockbox, nestled safely under his bed. He kicked at it with his heel, remembering its importance and it gave a reassuring metallic clunk.

Muffled words filled his ears. He picked out a few.

'Dementia', 'going downhill,' and 'not long now,' all did not fill him with hope.

There was a man too, out of focus, talking at him.

He could not make out much more, so decided to stare out of this window instead. The view wasn't much better here than in his chair in the hobby room outside.

Same old garden. Same dead plants. Same rain.

He heard people leave his room, and again, the sound of silence became deafening.

Chapter Thirty-Six

By the time I reached the building that housed my storytelling old matey, my mood had shifted very much to the positive. The earlier thoughts of sci-fi fantasy had brought heroic visions and possible storylines flooding my imagination.

I should write a book one day.

Maybe a funny exploits memoir where the dashingly heroic and downright hilarious officer saved all of the days.

The publishers would be literally fighting over the rights for the book, showering me with cash from wheelbarrows brought in by eager publishing apprentices.

If you haven't guessed, I can go off on tangents and get a bit excited.

Back in the real world reception, I looked about for my little mate but he was not in his regular spot. Melody was, however, and I noticed that she was eating a rather nice-looking jaffa cake from the pocket of her smock. I don't know if it's called that, but it sounded nursie. Shoving the whole thing in one go and not eating it in the correct manner of nibbling the outside bit and then scoffing the middle made me think a bit less of Mel. There are rules in life that you should just follow. Or chaos and bedlam ensues. Like never going to the shops in your pyjamas unless there is a medical emergency, or wearing dark socks with shorts. Oh, the mayhem.

She waved over to me smiling a crumb-covered welcome and beckoned me over. A worried look was hidden beneath the faux pleasantries though which I picked up with ease. A copper's nose and eyes are the bestest.

"Is everything okay?" She said once more.

Sigh

"Yes Mel, all good," I told her. "Where's G-Man?" I'm so hip and trendy sometimes that it astounds even me.

"He's just gone in with the doctor. He had a funny turn as you were walking here so we wanted to get him looked over to see if he was on the mend." She actually looked hopeful, so I wasn't going to break her little bubble that dementia isn't cured by antibiotics and a lemon slice.

"You mean to see if his condition has levelled out a bit?" She computed the words and chose to move on as if her brain slipped into no-function mode.

"No, not the brain, his heart had a murmur of something, but I hope he's okay. He's a kind old man. Never any trouble. You're welcome to chill out for a bit here if you want?" She opened the biscuit tin and the solitary Nice biscuit inside did not a warm welcome make.

"I best not. Crime might happen, you know."

She shrugged in a 'suit yourself,' but friendly motion and fished out another gleaming golden cake of purest jaffa from her smocket. (That's a smock's pocket. That's what they are called right? If not, they are now). The barbarian then shovelled it in, and again, her esteem points went down a tad.

Turning to leave, I felt a sudden rush of cold.

Something ran up my spine as the aforementioned shiver danced a jig on my grave.

It was enough to stop me in my tracks and look back, firstly at the nursing staff and then at the weather outside for the cause, which neither could be deemed as the culprit.

I stepped closer to the exit.

Another shiver.

What the actual fuck? I thought, disturbed by the feeling.

I considered what health problems could bring on such a weird feeling, lifting my arms to see if I was having some sort of stroke.

Shaking my head at my stupidity, I took another few steps.

"Stay."

Chapter Thirty-Seven

"Stay!" The voices screamed in unison. Back in control, they craved the last story to be told as that one was going to be the one to break everything.

"You cannot leave! You must hear the next tale!" They shouted silently outward towards the crack and then to the living world outside the void. Whilst no one could hear them from the tomb, all amassed heard the shouts.

They needed Alex to listen, to feel the pain of the next story.

Plans were quickly coming to The All. Should they try and keep him here, or bring him back as soon as possible to Gerald's side? Their thoughts became chaos in the darkness, fighting for supremacy, tearing at each other trying to be heard.

All the while, the child watched. And waited.

Hatred filled the blackness and The All settled on a course of action. Whilst it had never been in any of the amalgamated masses,' past, they knew they had to use the skills they now knew all too well. It was a bitter taste in formless mouths, but they wanted revenge, they existed purely for it.

If he leaves there will be consequences.

We will kill again.

We will kill them all.

Chapter Thirty-Eight

Four more days.

Ninety-six hours.

Five thousand seven hundred and sixty minutes.

Not that Detective Chief Inspector Boone was counting. He had done his thirty years and was tired. Drained by the mouthy scrotes too big for their boots. Exhausted by the political hurdles he'd had to face later in his career.

A glowing one it was though, ranging from desk sergeant to neighbourhood governor to inspector at New Scotland Yard. He had seen everything and done more. Now, for the last few years, he'd been plodding through whatever department kept his pension safe. There was little need to risk it as he had a nice little nest egg ready and waiting.

In four more days.

Ninety-six hours.

"Good night Tracy," he said as he moved through the large glass doors to the lift in the central column of the new building. She was a great staff officer and would make a great Superintendent one day in the shining beacon of the Metropolitan police they both loved so much. It was a family away from family, a home from home. Never a job like it, and never again.

In four days.

The thought brought a smile to his face and a weight lifted from his chest and shoulders. He felt lighter and the spring in his step had brought him out of the building into the night air.

The air was a lot cooler out here and Boone zipped up the blue fleeced jacket he always wore. It was getting a little old now, but then, he mused, 'weren't we all'?

The late hour brought the regular commuters, rushing from the coffee shop to the turnstiles in the race to get home before others. The invisible finish line was in front of everyone as they hustled and bustled through the old tube station.

It was a mix of decrepit and refurbished, the epitome of an architectural plaster. But each crack and metal framework pointed Boone homeward. He smiled again, realising that he would only need to do this for three more trips after this. Westminster to Waterloo, then onward to the leafy Surrey suburbs and home.

Getting down to the platform, he moved to his regular spot at the far left of the platform. He still loved to feel the whoosh of the oncoming tube as it hurtled from tunnel to platform. He would always watch the people pile out, a sea of commuting.

With three minutes till the next train, Boone pulled the telegraph from his satchel, skipping through anything non-police related.

A cold breeze brushed past the back of his neck and brought an involuntary shiver. The draft felt like delicate fingers brushing his neck, leaving the hairs there standing on end. He rubbed at it to warm himself, knowing the nearest person to him was twenty feet away.

The punch came without warning.

It hit him square in the back and felt immediately

like he'd been stabbed as the pain began to scream throughout his body like an electrical current, streaking a lightning bolt of sheer agony.

He tried to open his mouth to shout out, involuntarily through the shock of it, but he was rooted in place. He was still holding the newspaper, but his hands became fists and it crumpled in them.

For what felt like an age, he was stuck there, the pain reaching even the furthest parts of his body from the punch.

Boone tried to take stock of what was happening and he concluded, through the agony, that he was having a heart attack.

But this was nowhere near as described. No pain in the arm, no early warning signs.

The pain brought tears to his face which had reddened, and dampened with sweat. The pressure of the blood coursing through him brought a migraine-like pain, clouding his vision.

A sickening crunch within his chest that sounded like breaking twigs filled his ears, joined by a wet feeling on his shirt.

The dawning of what was happening, couldn't be happening, played havoc in his mind as, still unable to move but looking down as best he could, the material of the fleece moved.

His chest pushed out from within, stretching the skin, threatening to burst forth as he felt his heart thrust forward from the safety of its biological home.

The dark stain grew as Boone felt the skin of his chest

stretching, moving, undulating as his heart was forcibly pushed out of his chest from behind. The protective ribs cracked under the pressure bringing blood coursing up Boone's throat.

As he toppled forward, he was allowed a final, gurgled scream, muffled only by the screeching brakes of the tube train.

Onlookers turned in time to see the once proud Chief Inspector shattered by the force of the oncoming metal juggernaut.

The vision would remain in the minds of all onlookers, agonisingly scratched into a recurring memory.

*

Except for the woman, who nobody saw. No one could have realized that she was the cause of the carnage.

And as she drifted away from the chaos she had caused, she smiled.

Happy with her work.

Chapter Thirty-Nine

The phone rang at six-thirty a.m. that morning. I wasn't due at work. It was supposed to be a nothing day. To rest my aching everything. No thoughts of criminals. No thoughts of who's done what to whom. No emails from angry residents about their next-door neighbour but one having noisy parties.

It was the skipper. I immediately knew something had happened. It was something terrible. Something was horribly wrong.

"Morning Alex. I'm so sorry to wake you on your rest day, but didn't want you to hear this from the news'".

'Fuck. What's happened?' I thought, as my stomach looped. Painful scenarios went through a tick list of chaos in my mind and I spun around to make sure Claire was safe. Luckily, and somewhat obviously she was, so returned my attention to the call.

"Your old Guv, John Boone had a heart attack on the way home last night. I'm so sorry, Alex. I know you had a personal history with him. He was your first governor wasn't he?"

I tried to confirm in the affirmative, but my words were cracking on me. Not something I was used to as you can probably tell. I then felt hands around me, the warmth of a loving Claire bringing the world back into full colour.

How she knew was beyond me, but she was there, again, when I was crumbling.

Strength renewed, I answered.

"Yes, skip. That he was. A fucking decent bloke he is. Was. Sorry."

Realising I'd just sworn, technically, in front of the skipper made me feel a bit sheepish. It was like I'd let my professionalism guard down too much. I knew I always bordered on unconventional at the best of times, a maverick cool, dashingly hilarious vicar if you like. But I did not swear.

"Don't worry Al, totally understand. When you're next in, we'll go out and have a coffee. I never knew him, but only heard good things and if he had any hand in making you the officer you are today, then he is a fucking decent governor too." We bonded a bit that morning over the loss of one of the good ones. A distant family member everyone loved.

The feeling of loss for a colleague is an indescribable and profound emotion that transcends the boundaries of the workplace. It's a poignant mix of sorrow, nostalgia, and a deep sense of emptiness. When a colleague departs, whether through retirement, a new job opportunity, or the unfortunate event of passing away, the void they leave behind is not only in the office but in our hearts as well. Their absence is a constant reminder of the value they brought to our professional lives, the camaraderie we shared, and the daily interactions that created a sense of belonging. The memories and moments we spent with them become cherished treasures, and their absence serves as a sombre reminder of the fleeting nature of our time together in the ever-evolving world of work.

It was a sad day.

Saying my thanks and goodbyes, I laid down, held Claire, and wept.

Chapter Forty

It was a few days before I began to feel myself again. Chief Inspector Boone had had a profound effect on my life and while we weren't close currently, I knew he was still there. I knew that if I called, he would be of any assistance I could need. He was a helper. A man dedicated to the progress of the world around him. So if I needed him, he'd still help, offering the best of advice.

He'd be there.

Except, now... he never would.

Struggling after the death of a colleague is a solemn and challenging journey. The loss creates a palpable void, one that's felt not only in the workplace but also in the hearts of the team. Grief can be all-consuming, making it difficult to focus on daily tasks and goals. It's a journey through a landscape of sorrow and memories, where moments of shared laughter and collaboration are juxtaposed with the harsh reality of their absence.

However, I felt a determination to press forward, to be a tribute to the legacy of the departed inspector and an embodiment of their resilience. It's not an easy path, but it's one marked by resilience, unity, and the enduring impact of our colleague's contributions to our lives and work. Now that lifeline was gone. Is gone. He's gone. I kept trying to lift myself, to be a beacon for Boone, but I kept slipping back into the dark sadness loss brings and the world itself felt a little darker for his departure. He had taught me that every action causes a reaction and if you could pay it forward in a good way, it could make lives better.

It didn't even need to be kept in the family too! Helping

strangers was sometimes better, as they often did not expect it, so the feeling of goodwill was greater still. In my mind, the 'helped,' would then go off and assist others, spiralling outward till the help network would make the world a better place. Even if it was just a local phenomenon, I hoped that it would become a chain of events that brought about smiles throughout.

Was it a pipe dream? What was the harm in hope?

I don't know if he'd swallowed a trite quote book of management phrases but it had become my code of honour, my life mission. This badge of goodness drove me to leave behind a life that touched others for the better.

"What we leave behind will be a good, helpful life." I said to myself that morning. What we leave behind… Boone had left, helping no more. I know it's one of those motivational memes, but CI Boone had helped me beyond what he should've. I was young in service and on scene with a difficult crime scene. There had been a pretty grizzly murder that morning in my beloved Kingston and I was tasked with setting up an initial crime scene with the flimsy tape provided. I would be in charge of all crossings and had to keep a log of all badge numbers.

The flats above me were off limits as we were awaiting the crime scene officer to go in and check for evidence after the bodies within were rushed to hospital before life was pronounced extinct later that morning.

I'd tried to help a gent who needed to feed his cat, so thought nothing of letting him inside the block. He waved at me and I felt that I had done a service to the resident, confirmed by him shaking my hand in thanks as he left.

My life went to crap for a few days after that. I'd let a possible suspect get away, doubtful though it was in this instance. The Chief Inspector continued to throw 'what if though,' at me for a week.

Never again would I do that, and the inspector had stood his ground for me. My life changed thereafter, vowing to be better for everyone, a new, better version ready to mark my mark. I drifted through my thoughts, lost in the mood of events past.

*

There was no work today.

I'd become quite bored.

So my thoughts were stewing on the world around me.

I needed a reboot, a distraction from the dire.

Claire was working from home today though and even she was getting a bit miffed with my constant interruptions.

An offer of tea here, a biscuit there, a quick shag on the stairs before her Zoom meeting about finance/budget analysis. I found it amazing that she had managed to get herself into the beacon of respectfulness she was known for, at least from the waist up. I chuckled as she sat back down, looking demurely presentable for the camera, whilst table down, a sweaty mess in old comfy joggers.

As the meeting began, obviously off camera, I'm not stupid, I gave her the hilarious cock helicopter to make her giggle. I almost burst out laughing as I saw her face light up as the meeting began and everyone's screens blinked into life, her cheeks blushing from the view past the laptop.

I know. Hilarious. I'm a regular comedic mastermind.

But now I was bored again, having been shooed from the room.

I didn't want to be left with my thoughts and having sex on Zoom 'could get us both fired Alex!'

So off I slouched, like a spoiled petulant child who'd just been told off again to find where my pants had landed.

This was going to be a new week I thought to myself having woken up and realising I had nodded off into a post-sex nap. Life keeps moving and people will still need help.

I'll do it for Boonie.

The next set of shifts were lates. And when I say lates, I mean eleven to eight o'clock pm. So not late late, but later. I much preferred the morning shifts as I tend to potter at home and annoy Claire mainly when she's trying to do proper work.

So I left early.

There was a promise of a coffee after all.

I had hoped that it was one of the poncey ones the skipper usually didn't buy me. Made from coffee beans that were planted by Swedish virgins, delicately brought to the cup in their ample cleavage. Each bean delivered with an angelic soundtrack.

That was probably too far, but you get my drift.

Posh coffee. No instant crap for me today!

Chapter Forty-One

In the depths of the dark abyss, The All plotted from the profound and unsettling void as it stretched infinitely into the unknown. It was a place where all light and life were swallowed by obscurity, where the silence was oppressive and the coldness unforgiving. For years, the collected minds were left to wander in the endless expanse, searching for any glimmer of hope or clarity amidst the impenetrable darkness.

But now, there was a way out. There was a saviour. She would lead The All to the light.

Their plan was moving forward. They needed the officer here to hear the stories, and this murder would drive him to Gerald.

It was an abhorrent thing to do, but there was no choice for the amalgamated masses at this point and they did not want to get trapped here eternally when the old man died.

"He will come now. Nothing is stopping him from coming now." They said in unison, moving their awareness to the boy. Hatred bubbled up for him and their collected rage enclosed his meagre space further.

He whimpered formlessly which pleased all gathered.

"Aren't you happy that it will soon be over? Maybe we'll keep you alive to watch what happens next," they continued.

Because they knew, that if more stories were not told, there would be more deaths.

"We are The All and punishment was coming to the guilty."

Chapter Forty-Two

'It was going to be a tough day,' thought the forty-year-old woman as she rose from her bed. Sergeant Jess McClaren rubbed at her face, brushing sleep from her aching eyes. The night had been a tough one and she'd laid awake going through words she would say and more so how she would say them. She wasn't the best at showing care and attention at the best of times due to her father in the main.

She had moved from military base to base in her younger years, forming the strict discipline she was now benefiting from. It had given her the drive to work, the drive to succeed and lead.

Always expected to follow the armed forces route, her teen years brought conflict and arguments as her sexual longing reared its head. Never one to fall for the male of the species, she hid her true feelings deep within.

She was regimented, authoritative and stern, and she fell headlong in love with the total opposite. The strictness and discipline of her lifestyle were in complete contrast to the whimsy and gleeful abandon of Sarah.

Jess had bumped into her on a trip to London and was immediately captivated by the beauty of the flowing grace of the busker in front of her. She sang her song directly to Jess,' heart as the escalator slowed metaphorically under the lyrical spell. She seemed to hang there on the metal step for a romantic eternity, never wanting the beautifully held note to end.

To her, Sarah was the abandonment of regime, the definition of playfulness, encapsulating everything different to the stoic outlook Jess had only known.

She was a waterfall over a jagged rock face, and with each day, those hard points eroded.

Their paths were intertwined from then on, unable to leave one another. Each would bring the other closer in line with themselves, becoming the best parts on offer.

Sarah was saved from her unintentional spiral and Jess was allowed to see the beauty in things. But the army-focused father had not approved one iota.

He said that it was because she was not suited to army life, not regimented enough with no focal point of service.

She had taken it to mean that he was against her being a lesbian and they had fought. The battle would end up alienating both parents and siblings, with Jess leaving and joining the police force a year later. Sarah had followed her, ending up committing herself wholeheartedly to this warrior of a woman.

Still together today, Jess looked down at the woman she adored, getting up as quietly as she could to begin her day.

She planned to get in early as her boots needed a fresh shine and her white shirt with fresh crease lines. She never travelled in 'half blues,' as that was not the done thing, against the rules for the safety of officers. Some less controlled officers had gone against the guidance and had come a cropper when an incident unfurled in front of them. So she stuck to the rule, as she did all of them.

The train journey in was uneventful thankfully, as she needed to compose herself for her meeting with Alex. She laid out lines in her head ready to recite, which she hoped would help the older man.

'I know how you must be feeling'.

'I understand you're upset'.

'Do you need any time off?'

She did care for Alex, as she did for all officers under her wing, although she didn't show it as emotion. She viewed him as a little unconventional at times, but he would always get emails of thanks from individuals he dealt with and he was an officer she could trust, one that could be counted on.

Jess pushed him to do his skipper's exam on multiple occasions, but apparently, Alex was happy where he was and she didn't understand the lack of drive one bit but was happy to keep him as a ward officer. As did his residents to be honest.

Upon arrival, Alex was already in the office. He wasn't due to start for an hour but was there with his feet already under the desk. She noted that he was idly scrolling through various police platforms, clearly not absorbing the scrolling images and text in front of him.

"Alex," she said, trying not to sound as official as she normally did. She consciously softened her tone, aiming for approachable but still in charge, but the preprepared lines from earlier felt hollow and empty.

"Let's go grab a coffee?"

Chapter Forty-Three

Why the hell did I get changed? I knew I was going out for a chat. For effs sake. Now I had to go down into the clothing dungeon and get my normals on again.

My mind was all over the shop still. Turmoiled and troubled.

Getting rechanged, unchanged, dechanged(?) I went back to Jess who was still in plain clothes. The epitome of the phrase. Her nondescript black suit trousers and a light blue blouse were totally in character for the skipper, but I was not to judge.

I had worn my old Spiderman T-shirt and jeans combo that I was always comfortable in. My man-child personality was still clutching to superhero fantasies, but I didn't care. With what we deal with in the police, it was nice to switch off the brain and watch heroes save the day against fictitious villains.

'Not all heroes wear capes,' went the line. And I could name them! Spiderman was a particular fave as the nerd in him appealed to the geek in me. I loved seeing the good guys win as it reaffirmed my faith in humanity. Except for that one movie which I still to this day, cannot watch without a cuddle from Claire.

Damn you, Thanos.

We left the building and travelled to the coffee shop of the skipper's choosing. I wasn't fussy. Okay, I'm lying. I wanted one of the expensive ones she brought in from Tristan the wanky bespoke beverage barista.

I was actually a little excited about which one it was she normally went to, as I generally grabbed a quickie from Costa. (Other chains are available).

"You normally go here, don't you Alex?" she said as we reached the aforementioned purple palace. My heart sank a little bit and tried to rescue the situation.

"We can go wherever you prefer, skip!" That'll do it. Gentlemanly offering her the choice of establishment.

Shit.

She's a lesbian. What's the process here? Have I offended her? Crap. Fuck. Crap. I was definitely off as my mind was swearing up a good un.

'Keep them in you head Alex', I reminded myself.

"Or here's fine!" I blurted, gesturing quickly to the coffee house nearest.

Saved it. I think. Second guessing everything it seems.

I had nothing against her choice of partner whatsoever, I just got caught in a loop of not upsetting people. Sarah was a legend too. I met her a few times at meet-ups and ceremonies and we got on like a house on fire, mainly because I could embarrass the skipper with gigglesome stories to riotous laughter. I like making people happy, I may have mentioned it.

"We can go here Al, no worries." Al? Was she trying to be more friendly? She'd never called me that before. Not sure I liked it. 'Yeah, fine Je,' I thought to say back.

Balls, I suddenly thought, mustering a smile back at her. This is the 'put him in a place of safety,' management tactic at play here, much to the possible annoyance of Tristan who had lost the sale of not one, but two, overly overpriced coffees.

The Swedish virgin's bean delivery system would have

to wait.

Story of my life.

We sat and talked for what seemed like ages, but ended up only being about thirty minutes. Still nice though as the pretence of rank was gone for those moments.

It was good to talk. It was also a good send-off for my old boss. I raised my drink as best I could to the old man due to the sodding stupid little handles the coffee mugs had.

Bring back flagons I say.

As we left, I heard the skipper audibly sigh in relief as this was not her forte at all. I think I had subconsciously realised this before coffee time so had tried not to break down and be a blubbery mess. I don't think she could've handled a grown man with a snot bubble.

In helping her, I had helped myself. Funny that.

Back at the office, Danny was ready and waiting.

Chapter Forty-Four

Danny was more fired up than he'd ever been. Coiled like a cobra, he was in the uniform of an officer ready to arrest anyone of note. His pockets included more than he would normally need with an overflow of various-sized evidence bags and other miscellaneous kits stuffed in every Metvest pocket.

It was a big day.

He would not let anyone go.

He had already checked on who the custody sergeant was and this was a skipper to not suffer criminals lightly. Known as a custody hard arse, this would almost guarantee a cell if Danny could find the right culprit.

'None of the reassurance bollocks for this aspiring young hero,' thought Danny as he stood up upon the entry of his sergeant. He was standing to attention in more ways than were obvious as his excitement and anticipation of the incoming shift grew.

He clocked something amiss as the skipper entered though as soon afterwards, Alex followed, both of them wearing plain clothes.

Was it an undercover day? 'Even better,' he thought.

"Morning Danny," the pair said, the skipper leading the greeting.

Neither seemed too rushed to get out on the beat, the shift starting in mere moments. 'They must be fucking,' the young officer surmised. He made a note to keep an eye on the pair as he could easily raise a grievance using this newly uncovered evidence. He planned out how he would use this information to move both out of his way so that he could prove his trustworthiness to the Senior Leadership Team.

He smiled to himself, running career options through his head, thinking how this could benefit his journey through the ranks.

The skipper's voice brought his train of thought crashing back to reality.

"I checked the overnights and there were two robberies, one seemingly having been committed by James Redburn, who is wanted for shoplifting and assaulting PC Jane Worthy. We want to catch him for sure. Keep them peeled during your Town Centre patrols today guys".

He immediately became Danny's target.

"Sgt, can I grab a car and take some calls then? Hopefully I can catch him." Even though he wasn't a response driver, he knew enough to get him through traffic faster than normal drivers.

"No Dan, foot patrol, please. Local businesses need some reassurance and it's a good idea to show presence. Can you both wear your high-vis jackets?"

To Dan, it was a dagger through him. He hated looking so exposed, so, so yellow. This was not a job for his standing.

The anger grew in him and the anticipation was crushed underfoot.

He would still get his body, but this skipper was holding him back. When he got back to the office he would write a strongly worded email to the inspector to get him to where he deserved.

The two officers got ready for the shift ahead, Alex transferring epaulettes and sliders to the brightly fluorescent overjacket. The older officer noted that Danny had rolled his up to be carried on the utility belt.

'Not what the skipper had asked,' but at least he had it on him, thought Alex.

Danny led the way to the yard and the two officers strode out, neither ready for what they would face.

Neither were ready for the dramatic turn of events to come.

Chapter Forty-Five

Death is not known for its patience and the amalgamated masses had been imprisoned long enough. They thought that one, had hoped that one, would be enough but the push was not enough.

Not wanting to kill is a fundamental expression of humanity, rooted in an innate capacity for empathy and compassion. Normally, the desire is to preserve life, even in the face of adversity or conflict, as it is a testament to the moral and ethical evolution of a species.

Whether it pertains to the aversion to taking another human life or a commitment to the preservation of all living creatures, this inclination to avoid harm reflects the aspiration to find peaceful resolutions, foster understanding, and build a more harmonious world. It reminds us that the path to a better future lies in our ability to embrace non-violent alternatives, promote empathy, and seek common ground in the pursuit of a more just and humane society.

But this luxury was for the living. This was not for The All. They were long past this moral notion now.

Drastic measures needed to be taken.

This action would make him hear Gerald's next tale.

The next story would be told and he would listen.

He would remember.

He will know.

PC Alex Chambers would know his part in all this.

Drifting like a ghost, the amalgam let its lead personality free once more and it pushed through the ever widening crack. Each day, it became easier to leave and whilst still tethered to the host, their strength grew.

Each step seemed to echo faintly, much like the fading whispers of moments long gone. Shadows danced on the periphery of consciousness, and they drifted through the bustling world outside. A spectre of their former selves, they found solace, a refuge from the cacophony of death and pain, allowing them all to focus, to explore the depths of what they had become, like a ghost lingering in the realm between reality and reverie.

They would tell the world the stories.

He would know what he has done.

And he will break.

And they would know what has been left behind.

Chapter Forty-Six

This shit shift was dragging. Nothing was happening. Even the radio was dead.

The Immediate Response Vehicles were silent, yet to be awoken from their slumber by the bark of calls. Response officers began taking arrest inquiries to stay proactive. Other local neighbourhood teams started spontaneously cuppa-ing with a copper to look busy. As soon as the officers had left the base, they split to cover more streets where Danny hadn't spoken to a soul. He hadn't been approached either as his external demeanour screamed 'Don't fucking talk to me'.

It was Danny's idea to solo today so he could answer calls that didn't come. He stomped around and around, covering the same streets without any public interaction, circling like a predator. No residents or businesses were reassured by the fire-faced officer. Finally breaking his route, he went into the local Tesco Express on the corner of the busy one-way system.

He vaguely remembered that this location was where the other young officer was assaulted by the drugged-up shoplifter, Redburn.

Streets away, Alex was deep in thought.

*

I felt I should've gone with the young whippersnapper today but with everything still hanging over me, I thought some fresh air and nice chats would keep my mind off things. Nice chats with residents and businesses mind you, as Danny was not the inspiring conversationalist I needed today.

So I was glad that he had suggested soloing.

I was still flip-flopping emotionally, but holding it together, but I wasn't ready one bit for Krystal from Anne Summers though. That was a bit much for me today, so I resigned myself to an amble, a wander around, speaking to inoffensive people and passing the day.

Yes. That's the way.

No drama.

I'll pop by Gerald's tomorrow and catch up with the old-timer. That would be a nice distraction, I thought, wondering if he would spill another of his excellent fables. Tomorrow though, reassurance today.

*

The local Tesco store was bustling with people running to collect the various items of produce they needed. The hustle and bustle of regular shoppers were like insects to Danny right now, their insignificance an annoyance at best.

He glanced at them with contempt born of frustration but it was when he entered the drinks aisle that the crash reverberated around the shop. Glass skittered and heads turned towards the sound, as Danny rounded the corner, his interest suddenly perked.

The red liquid began to seep across the floor, spreading outward from the incident Danny now saw.

*

With Danny still out of sight and mind, I still felt a bit lost, but was beginning to drag myself back to my normal level of giddy optimism and blind hope. I'd promised myself to get back to the jokes and funny stories soon, eager to lift my spirits.

Tomorrow's another day. I will most definitely get there.

*

The red liquid disappeared under the shelving unit as it spread around the light-tiled floor. The scarlet fluid turned the white flooring pink as it continued its oozing journey outward, slowing now as momentum eased.

Danny traced the impact point to a smashed bottle of red wine.

People were also looking towards the crash and the person standing over it. He was dressed in shabby, dirty clothing, looking like he had slept in them for weeks. Stains mottled the fabric joining a mismatch of rips and tears.

The bottle had smashed at his feet, throwing red stains up his trouser leg to the knee. The grey jogging bottoms were smeared with days-old muck and in desperate need of either a wash or throwing away.

Danny wretched at the smell of the man and brought his hand to his face to try to mask the odour from assailing his nostrils. All thought of any politeness at not mentioning the odour was pushed firmly away by the filthy smell orbiting the man in front of Danny.

He looked at the face of the haggard man in front of him and as their eyes met, the police officer recognised the wanted face of James Redburn.

Danny knew what had to be done. He would arrest Redburn and get his name in lights, forever remembered.

This was his day.

Chapter Forty-Seven

I heard the radio crackle into life with a strident "URGENT ASSISTANCE!!" shouted over the airwaves. Numbers began assigning themselves to the call, asking for locations, and details.

"2, 1"

"2, 2"

There was an underlying panic, but hidden well under the authority of urgency.

Officers, including myself, defaulted automatically into a learned behaviour, readying ourselves for literally anything. I knew it was Danny though from voice alone, so took point on getting info.

"Dan, where are you mate?" I chose a tone of support but with enough punch to let him know help was coming. If we only knew where to fucking send it.

The radio was filled with sounds of a scuffle and I quickened my pace, looking around for anything or anyone that would give me a clue as to my colleague's whereabouts. Mere seconds had passed but it felt like the metaphorical lifetime people speak of. All I could think about was getting to Danny and helping, however I could. Whatever he was dealing with was above and beyond even his normal level of calamitous action.

His location was being triangulated as the seconds clanked on, my feet still marching towards an abyssal nothingness. I quickened my pace to a run, although without a destination, and began surveying the shops as I passed them for signs of chaos.

The radio's static crackled on again.

"Tess... Get the fuck off me!"

Silence once more.

Tess? What? What the actual??

'Dan, need more mate', I thought, panic levels rising.

Tesco! The local one on the corner.

Yes! And with that, I was off. As fast as feet and breath would allow as I explained where he was to units flooding the area. Through panting and exertion, I diverted everyone to what I was sure was Danny's location.

"Two minutes out!" chimed in '2 2,' as sirens began to fill my ears.

Other call signs followed but I would easily be first on the scene as, rounding the corner, could see people leaving the store at pace. Some onlookers were filming with their smartphones, pointing towards whatever macabre chaos my teammate was handling. They moved themselves to the windows of the store trying to film whatever was unfolding.

Don't help the guy, just fucking film it. Brilliant.

I flew into the store and passed staff and customers alike until I rounded the corner to see something from my worst fears.

Danny was being held in a headlock by James Redburn who I immediately clocked from the wanted poster on all the station walls. The eyes of the wanted man were frantic, struggling to hold the younger officer tightly around the neck. Danny's hands kept slipping, wet from some fluid as yet unknown, and he kept grasping at Redburn's locked arm. Both men were desperate for different reasons but James managed to keep both Danny and a bottle of wine firmly grasped.

"Get the fuck off me!" Danny shouted again, more forcefully than the last, as he flailed backwards with an extended asp, striking everywhere, hitting little.

Redburn was yet to see me, so I approached quickly, but with the thought to try and calm the situation for both parties,' benefit initially. If ten seconds of that failed, I'd fling my full body weight into a disruptive slam to knock them both over.

Tactics ran through my head, unknowns throwing spanners in each plan.

Did he have a knife?

How did they get to this point?

There was no time for anything though.

The panicked suspect looked up at me and screamed.

Chapter Forty-Eight

It wasn't in anger, but abject terror.

It threw me to be completely honest. I'd never had that effect on anyone before this moment.

Another scream.

What the hell was happening?

He was now pointing the bottle in my direction, adrenaline seemingly giving him the strength to hold Danny even more tightly around the neck. His eyes bulged in fear, almost staring through me.

"Get back devil!" Screamed Redburn.

Danny made his move. He struck out at his captor with his asp, catching him on the outstretched arm, causing it to fly backwards. Dazed, his grip loosened enough for Danny to begin to free himself. A flicker of hope-filled us both at this minor win.

Redburn was almost hiding behind Danny now, no longer his captor, more so his shield, protecting him from me for some ungodly reason.

Only seconds had passed but the sounds of sirens had grown stronger, with cars skidding to a halt outside.

Redburn had nowhere to go.

His panicked eyes searched for anything that could help, but all he could see around him were the regular shop fittings and produce you would expect.

Boot leather slapped outside as help arrived.

The smash of the bottle echoed throughout the store, its strident destruction clear over the cacophony of chaos.

Danny froze, unable to move as the broken bottle was levelled with his neck, exposed through the struggle.

The jagged glass cut easily into Danny's throat and I burst inside. I was moving towards them both as blood jetted from the wound. It had dug deep into an artery that was clear from the amount of blood spouting from the gashed neck.

Danny went limp and clawed at the injury, desperately trying to hold in his lifeblood. The look he gave me, of both panic and despair, would stay with me.

Redburn dropped him and took steps back, but I could only try and help Dan, knowing that I couldn't. Redburn would have to be dealt with by the other officers at this point, my thoughts and efforts only for Dan.

Pressure applied to the wound, I screamed orders to get an ambulance en route.

Officers were in the store now, running towards the three of us.

I looked up at Redburn, covered in Dan's blood. Blinking both blood and tears from my eyes I looked at the murderer of my colleague. He looked strangely calm now as he raised the sharded glass to his own throat and said;

"She won't get me…"

It was then that I heard myself scream as Redburn sliced the shard across his neck.

Chapter Forty-Nine

I... What happened? Oh god. I keep seeing it.

Over and over.

How do I get past this?

It's in my eyes. The vision. The blood.

What seemed like days had passed since Danny's death.

His murder.

I felt like part of me was still there, stuck in an endless scream. I could see his face, Dan's I mean. Redburn was faceless at this point, no longer needed in my memory, blocked to be a barrier to further pain. I remember Claire, being there. Always. She was such a rock, the stability to my confusion. She had helped me through the initial chaos after the incident.

It was a blur for me though.

Blocking a painful memory is like burying a treasure chest in the depths of one's consciousness. It's a subconscious act of self-preservation, an instinctual defence against the emotional tempest that certain recollections can unleash. In the intricate corridors of our minds, we stumble upon these locked doors, guarding the most traumatic chapters of our lives.

The mind, in its wisdom, understands that not all memories should be easily accessible. Just as we shield our eyes from a blinding sun, we shield our hearts from the searing pain of the past. It's a form of self-compassion, a shield against the relentless assault of anguish.

Yet, this act of blocking is not without its complexities. While we may successfully hide a memory from our conscious awareness, it continues to exert its influence in subtle and often insidious ways.

The moment Danny died, he had looked at me in sheer undiluted terror, before the realisation, and the pain had hit him. I continue to see his face convulsing into an agonised expression before his life left him, and then all energy, movement, and future dissolved into nothingness. His blood-filled throat gurgled an inaudible cry that no one could make out.

His skin seemed to become more greyer, a shadowed husk of the aspiring young man.

Officers had run into the chaotic store to help all three people, most to their fallen family members, some to Redburn. It was quickly established that both people were deceased, far removed from any earthly help.

Statements and witnesses were quickly gathered, Body Worn Video was saved for evidential purposes. The duty inspector quickly deduced that there was nothing that I could've done, although I questioned myself throughout the coming days.

I should've done more. Danny would've still...

No. I can't. Everyone had said that even if I went straight to Redburn and not paused for the mere moments I did, I still would not have stopped Danny from being killed.

A few days afterwards, I had tried to come back to work, but the sergeant was ready having had a call from Claire that I had forced myself in. Waiting at the gates was one of our 'Blue Light Champions', officers tasked with helping their teammates get through times like I was facing. I admired their work, but never thought I'd be a recipient of it. They strove to help not only the physically injured but also the mentally.

Jess was also there.

Sorry... Scratch that.

The skipper was also there. I'm forgetting myself.

"Go home Al. You're signed off till you're ready mate." The calming tone had a stern undercurrent that she wasn't going to take no for an answer. There was care on her face but also a clear underlying expression of wanting to hug me, although I wasn't sure whose benefit it was more for.

She was holding back tears. And failing.

We exchanged hollow pleasantries, I'm not sure, I can't remember the words, but it ended with me leaving. I walked off, away from the station to see where my feet would take me.

*

It felt like an hour, pacing and wandering. But when I checked my watch, it was just enough time to bring me to a certain old man's window.

I locked eyes with Gerald as I walked up the path to his care home.

I wasn't sure which one of us looked more emotionally broken.

Melody, the nice nurse from the other week was here, smiling inanely at me. I didn't feel very melodic though and it was plainly on my face.

"Having a bad day Mr Policeman?" She asked, with actually some care in there. Not enough to remember my name mind... but at least she recognised my sans uniform. I thought for a second about unloading but I didn't think she would be able to comprehend what I've been through. It also wasn't fair for the general public to hear what officers go through. We were supposed to reassure the masses, not terrify them.

It's a shame.

Officers go through everyone's worst days. That's their lives. Constant misery. No one ever calls us and says 'No bother, everything's great. Keep on going!'

I felt emotion bubbling up, a mix of sadness and anger, the beginnings of tears forming.

I'll fluff an answer.

"I... yes. Bad day. Work. Hay fever." In my current mental state, that was as close to 'nailed it,' as I was going to get.

"Oh. Sorry to hear that. Are you hear to see Gerald? I'll get you both some tea." A light at the end of the tunnel, however small.

Nodding, I went over to the old man.

I hoped he would either tell me a tale or just sit there so I could tell mine.

Chapter Fifty

It had felt like forever since he last saw sunshine. 'But it wasn't going to be today either,' thought the elderly man as he sat staring out into the rain.

Gerald sat staring out of the window most days. He couldn't remember first sitting down. Couldn't even remember where the window led to.

It was outside. Where though, he didn't know that either.

The chair seemed as old as the frail man sitting there, staring into the murky depths of the poorly maintained garden. Gerald shifted his aching bones as he thought about the day ahead of him.

The garden outside had died long ago, the plants long perished due to no one tending to their meagre needs. They had withered and shed whatever life they had in them before Gerlad's mind rewound to.

He longed to die with them.

The emptiness was a crushing ache within him, but he felt like he was being held in the stasis of monotony for a reason as yet unknown.

He realised that a piano was playing somewhere in the hobby room. The melodic sound had a crackle to it so he deduced that it was from a pre-recorded source. The delicate piano notes were joined by a softly sung vocal which Gerald's hearing was struggling to pick out.

"And the vision, that was planted in my brain, still remains" came one undistorted lyric that old ears heard over the normal room sounds.

Gerald was then aware of a man sitting next to him. It was the police officer, Alex Chambers, number SW183. This name and number was in his mind for some reason, a clarity in the fog, etched in his brain like a cancerous growth.

The mist of his dementia seemed to part and images that created a story moved and found their place in the incoming storyboard, ready to be told to the willing recipient.

Words followed, beginning to complete each chapter.

His mouth and mind were no longer under his control. He was now under the spell of the narrator, telling the story that urgently needed to be birthed.

The images that created the fable moved and found their place in the incoming tale, jostling with each other, excited to be unleashed into the world.

He will hear the story.

This one will bring focus.

'He will enjoy this one,' thought Gerald...

Torment

The last confession of Gerald Heggarty

1

Where.

Where to start? With my story? Or theirs? Hers?

Do I begin where it ends? Where I end?

We should, though, start with the rain.

Because it always seems to rain when we kill people.

We don't plan it that way, it just seems to happen. A fortunate fate. We call it a good omen because the closest we all came to getting caught was when it was sunny.

She caused that. The bitch was still trying to ruin my life. She had managed to take control as she was the catalyst for the rebirth. She birthed the amalgam.

My first kill came as a matter of self-defence. That's not strictly true, it was in sheer anger and more than a smidgen of curiosity from a youngling, but could be argued as self-defence in court m'lud. No one would believe a boy of ten years young would, or could be capable.

The old man had deserved it, though, well and truly, that was a fact beyond any rational argument. He had taken the blade like a trooper too, not even a scream was heard.

It took half the fun out of it.

I still remember the blood, as it got everywhere. Great

gouts of it spouting all over the shop! I had to wash away most of the evidence before I left the building, packing only what my small arms could carry. Some clothes and food, what money was in the house, and that chicken. Oh my. I still remember it.

Four people died that night.

I then became the second version of myself, a host to my darkness. One that could hide in the shadows more effectively, leaving all suspicion alleviated.

At this early point in my life, I kept mostly silent to not get caught. I would hide in the shadows when my dark urges arose, making sure when the accidents happened, I could not be the suspicious person left on scene.

Older years brought access to more resources and better still, easier prey. Being as nondescript as I was, I could hunt the cattle with greater ease.

I don't know where the need to kill came from, obviously, it was there from my beginning as there had always been a longing to see life end, even within my first memories. The urge to take life, to see it ebb away was something the mind wanted, not the boy. And it chipped away at my humanity, driving it further down into the shadowed recesses. I satiated my hunger with smaller animals, rats... cats... then the thrill, no, the need drove us onwards.

I was unleashed that night. Free to kill, to nudge people towards death.

The second main kill was also in self-defence. No. I can't. It was in utter anger and revulsion. I was fed up with her, she had served a purpose.

God. She went on and on, trying to drive me to

mischief. Me. It still makes me laugh to this day.

I mean, she did not know who she was fucking with. She knows now for certain, and I suppose I did end up with a bit of mischief when you think of it. I still keep a heartfelt memento of that kill under my bed. Happy times. It's amazing what you can preserve nowadays.

After that, I had to disappear again, become anew once more.

I learned though, practised my art. Got it down to a finessed final form.

Train stations always provide easy prey. While not exactly 'hands-on', it was more 'push off'.

There was one guy in Bournemouth if I remember, late nineties, I think. He certainly got a solid hit from that train, which I helped along. Didn't even know his name.

Like grinding cheese on a grater.

When the people jumped out of the train doors and saw the mess, I just joined the escaping throng and suspect one was gone.

Easy as that.

The stations were always ones where we knew there was no CCTV or platform staff to observe my kill. Without any evidence available, my subtle nudge as the murderous locomotive pulled in would be unsolvable.

Poisoning became fun too, watching people get sick and then perish from horrible symptoms. This was a slow way to do it, so did not fulfil the initial buzz of seeing the death stare, or the surprised look people got when they were unexpectedly, and sometimes brutally killed.

But it wasn't enough. I needed to feel the kill, as

nothing topped using a knife, or tools. The grind of a blade against the body. Oh my, just the thought of nicking an artery and watching the crimson fountain. I could bathe in its warmth.

So, this was me.

What do you think? Impressed that I've never been caught?

Probably just loathe the fact that I'm a brutal killer. We all have urges, mine are just a bit unique shall we say.

I don't care what you think though, I'm not doing this for fame or fortune. No book deal at the end of this for me.

I did it because it was fun.

But you're here to hear the story of the kill that changed everything aren't you…?

When I was almost caught?

Because of her, and her justice. This would soon become corrupted too, like everything I touch.

This is the story of the birth of the amalgam and my journey to this hell hole.

Thank you so much, Helen.

Bitch.

2

The warmth of the sun heated the day in early August. 2009 had brought many major events already and it was not yet finished.

More than four hundred Palestinians and four Israelis

were killed since fighting began the previous December. January brought an announcement from Israel about a unilateral cease-fire in Gaza with Hamas saying it would continue to fight as long as Israeli troops remained in the area.

For the first time in three hundred and forty-one years, a woman was appointed as poet laureate and the Williams sisters battled it out in the Wimbledon final.

The world was changing, evolving, growing even.

But not for the man who sat staring out of the window, hidden in the shadow, sunlight obscured by the heavy curtains. He watched the dust particles dance and float in that single beam, oblivious to the developing world around them.

New inventions seemed to come daily, and he felt left behind by it all. He was not bothered by it though. The things that he had seen were enough and he cared little for material things. He preferred to travel light, able to leave at a moment's notice if the need arose. He had his case ready and packed with the few possessions he loved though.

The room was sparsely decorated, a single painting of a wagon stuck in a winding river, the only sign that someone had put thought into the decor. He smiled at it, remembering. Mismatched seats filled the rest of the living room which doubled as a dining area.

A door led off into another darkened room which was the man's bedroom. It was often left unused as he would regularly lose consciousness to sleep in the very chair he occupied.

"I wish you had died long ago, you bastard," a female

said. "All this death would never have happened." There was scorn and hatred in the voice. It oozed pure malice, abhorrence born from pain.

"Fuck off." Was all he could retort.

In recent weeks, he'd been feeling less and less in control of his facilities. Like a ghost at the wheel. He'd wake up in the bedroom, having fallen into a dreamless sleep wherever he sat. He'd be lying there, on top of the covers in the traditional coffin manner, arms crossing his chest.

Was it a message? He shrugged off the ludicrous thought almost as quickly as it had arisen.

Another lapse brought actual pain as when cooking, he'd idly slice through one of his fingers preparing dinner. He remembered wincing at the pain as he bent the injured finger unconsciously. It had sent an electric jolt of pain up his arm and he had grabbed it as if the grasp would stop the injury causing more distress.

Hours always seem to slip by recently.

He'd sit in the morning to read his book or plan his next move and then it would be five... six o'clock. Days were lost, slipping through his hands like the metaphorical sands of time. He imagined time as an actual substance, and it was a thing he needed to keep physical control of. He tried grasping and grabbing at each grain but was failing at such an impossible task.

It was late in the day when the thump of music began.

He'd complained many times, mainly by hammering a broom on the ceiling. Holes proclaimed each report of protest. The anti-social fuckers from upstairs played their songs at deafening levels at random points, always a disturbance. With his cane, broom, or whatever was in reach, he would thud his annoyance to always no avail.

He had thought about killing them, planned it even. Slowly and painfully the neighbours would die, but his adage of 'never shitting on his own doorstep,' would be broken by such a delicious diversion.

'Follow the rules and stay hidden', he thought.

He wanted to kill them so badly though. That would be an exquisite vengeance alongside the normal thrill of the kill. Poisoning was an easy tactic and one that would be hard-pinned on the old man from downstairs.

"Go kill them. You want to. Do it."

Again she spoke. Urging him on. She knew he wanted to do it though and she was exactly right.

"Knife them" she oozed, pushing him to consider breaking his rules.

"Will you fuck off and leave me be!" Anger had risen in him. He was holding himself back now as his violent tendencies craved a new victim.

It had been too long.

He felt an all too familiar urge begin to rise.

He found himself agreeing with the voice in his head.

She knew what he wanted.

3

"Hello darkness my old friend..." came clearly through the floorboards as the classic from Simon and Garfunkel began another musical assault.

Whilst it wasn't the normal thud of heavy metal, the volume made each word clear in the small flat.

"I've come to talk with you again...

Because a vision softly creeping..."

He turned and pulled one of his limp pillows over his head, pressing down as hard as his old arms would allow. Even then, he could still pick out the delicate strings of the song as the melody flowed from the speakers in the rooms above. He felt that they were lying down on the floor above so that their music was directed straight at him.

More guitars followed and the overhead resident added to the cacophony by belting out a murdered version of the lyrics. Drunk, the male then started banging on the floor with his feet, an anti-social percussion of torment.

He wailed along, out of tune at almost every note.

The weary, tired man in the bed was feeling all of his sixty-seven years and the neighbours from hell were not helping his current retirement, but the anti-social nature of their existence only added to his feelings of encroaching caducity.

"Enough is enough isn't it? It's time to kill again."

She was not wrong.

As the song hit its crescendo, he plotted.

"And the sign flashed its warning...

In the words that it was forming..."

*

The next morning, it began at eleven. The old man had

been allowed sleep as the night's silence returned near three a.m. He awoke angry at the continued disturbance.

The song being blasted sounded to his old ears like some form of guitar-stringed torture. The thud-thud-thud-thud of the drums shook the room, sending waves through the small space.

He then heard the chorus rise and picked out the lines from the noise above that brought a wide smile to his face.

"It's been a long time comin', and the table's turned around

'Cause one of us is goin', one of us is going down..."

*

He didn't know where the knocking sound had come from, so scanned around. This was not his kitchen. He was outside his home, in a cluttered hallway. There was a broken bicycle near the stairs.

He was standing in front of a door, and he noticed that his fist had caused the rapping clunking sound of his hand on wood. Footsteps began approaching the door and, still in his striped pyjamas, the elderly man shuffled a step forward unconsciously.

He felt awake, but almost dreamlike, not fully in control of his actions. He was a passenger currently, being allowed to see what his body was doing.

The wood of the door flew open and a mountainous man appeared in the gap, filling it almost entirely. His face was covered in hair, long black curls met with the lengthy beard giving him the appearance of a large bear. The dark faded shirt bore a skeletal figure and the words 'iron maiden,' across the chest. It depicted a bony undead hand reaching out towards the old man now shadowed before it.

"What?" boomed the giant. He looked down upon the frail man in front of him and moved his head down to fit the level of the vulnerable little disturber.

Music bellowed from the room, louder now than heard from downstairs. The old man muttered something unintelligible.

"I can't hear you, you old sod. Fuck off." The colossal man moved a hand to shove the small decrepit individual away from his doorway, annoyed by the interruption.

The speed of the knife surprised both males.

It sliced the hulking mammoth across the neck and he immediately grabbed at the wound, mouth falling open. Blood jetted from the wound, filling the hallway with a torrent of crimson. Looking down, he saw a grin fill the elderly face, as red viscous fluid dripped from his hooked nose. The man watched in shock as the scarlet rivulets ran down the older face, flowing through the lines of his age.

He felt a further punch in his leg, then another on the opposite side. The blade had expertly punctured both arteries, causing the man to fall backwards, landing heavily on the floor behind him as his legs quivered out from under him.

He whimpered as the life drained from him, watching as the blood-drenched geriatric tottered off down the hall.

The last image he saw was the wide smile showing the yellow teeth of the aged.

4

The sirens began to fill his ears over the sound of the shower as he snapped back to reality. He looked down at his hands and saw the last vestiges of the blood run through his fingers, washing the sins of this morning away.

Music was still playing, but the sirens were getting clearer by the moment.

Panic began to set in. Where were the blooded clothes? The knife?

He stumbled out of the bathroom to find his suitcase packed, and ready to go as it always was. Next to it was a carrier bag filled with clothes dyed red with blood.

But no knife.

He stuffed the carrier bag into a second bag, throwing in the last of the coffee grounds he had to hopefully mask any smell from the acrid blood-soaked contents.

The panic drove him to hurriedly get dressed as the sirens ended with a screech of tyres somewhere at the foot of the block of flats.

Checking his case one last time and a cursory glance around, he left his home, hearing the thud of boots rushing up the stairs. Radios crackled and orders were barked as the officer flew past. He let the officers disappear and then trundled down, opting to overact the frailty of his years when in public spaces.

He was soon outside and away from the chaos he had somehow created.

*

In the safety of his flight, he saw another car arrive and from the boot, a young officer was grabbing items, hurriedly stuffing them into a black holdall. He then jogged hurriedly after an officer of some rank, his inspector maybe, towards the block of flats.

The older of the two went inside with the urgency born of duty, leaving the constable hurriedly pulling a reel of tape from his bag.

It was adorned with blue lettering proclaiming 'crime scene', a capitalised warning to keep clear.

It was then that the elderly killer began to fully remember the morning's attack and the final resting place of the knife.

He needed to retrieve it.

Never before had he left any evidence to his recall.

Always careful, always precise. It has been what has kept him free from prison all these years.

Carefully he approached the young man, thinking, and calculating his method of entry. He thought of angles he could take that would melt the heart of this new barrier to safety.

"Sir…" He cracked his voice, ramping up the vulnerability. "I need to feed my cat before you tape up this entry. I will then go to the shops while you investigate whatever has happened. It was such a nice neighbourhood."

The officer looked him up and down and quickly ushered him through, looking like he was tickling off an incident to-do sheet in his mind.

"Please do it and come straight back down. We're

probably only doing this as a precaution so it shouldn't be too long." His smile was filled with warmth and care behind the urgency, so much so that the old man had to check his surroundings, gathering himself in the process.

He nodded and walked past the young constable, patting him on the arm as a thank you.

The knife was located within minutes, the memory of its location aiding the quest. The bucket under the sink sloshed as it was pulled out, the cleaning products assailing his nose with a multitude of scents.

He wiped the blade dry and opened his case, finding a secure space next to his old lockbox.

"You're going to get caught, bastard! I've got you now!" screamed the woman's voice suddenly in his ear. He looked around, worried that the police officers above him heard the commotion and would come downstairs, finding him and his ferreted evidence.

No footsteps were heard apart from the shuffling of his own feet as he left this home for the final time.

The young officer waved him through and to keep the pretence, an elderly hand was offered in thanks. The young officer made sure to make eye contact but it was only briefly as he was still hurrying through his police processes.

The old man walked away from the scene he had caused. He walked away from this life and planned his next one.

He almost felt sorry for the officer as when he shook the older hand, he did it with care not to hurt the older man.

And in this brief exchange, he noted the name emblazoned across his uniform as PC Alex Chambers nodded his farewell.

Chapter Fifty-One

I'm going to piss myself today. There's no way around it. One of the golden rules John, shit, sorry, Inspector Boone would say, is never piss yourself in uniform.

But the tenth of August 2009 would forever be known as the day PC Alex pissed himself.

"It is something that does not inspire confidence in the uniform, Alex." Well duh. But what he meant was that as a Police Constable, you need to be aware of your limits. Open with a joke, and bring the nugget of goodness afterwards. Grab their attention and then say what you want to.

He's got a rule for everything, and they were all worth writing down to be fair. For someone as young in service as I was, he was God. I wouldn't be here without him. He's been a font of policing goodness in my first few years in the Met.

One time, (not at band camp, but a custody suite) I managed to get myself locked in the airlock without a badge. Oh, how we all laughed as I sat there for an hour before I was found.

Twat move, but I learned from it.

I learned from him.

I was the padawan to the Jedi Master and today, I was going to show him that his efforts were not in vain.

The call today was to a knife attack in a block of flats and the victim had multiple injuries. It was a third-floor block in a shitty part of town so units from across the borough were streaming to the area.

There was no way I was going to cock this up as all the brass would be looking.

Being second on scene, cordons would need to be put in and that's down to the newbie. I'm fine with that, mind. I'd rather guard a bit of tape than go see the grizzly mess upstairs. The guy was worse for wear which I know I should be hardened to, but it still hurts. Haven't seen that many as yet too. The bodies I'd been called to were generally the elderly who had died at home, not one carved up like this one. I don't think I was ready for that just yet.

I've been to so many people's worst days and every time I can't solve their case for whatever reason, I take it upon myself as a personal failure. Sometimes there's no evidence, or the CPS hasn't enough to charge, the list went on, but I tried to make sure I did my bit in the investigation process.

The car the Guv was driving rounded a corner at speed and, not gonna lie, it made me grin. I love blue light runs. Streaming through the traffic as they parted at the sound of the woo-woos and nee-naws. I feel I need to confess something though. Driving down the middle with cars on either side, always makes me feel like Luke Skywalker on his Death Star run.

Just without the Proton Torpedoes or any bullseyed womp rats.

Flying through the traffic will never get boring.

We screeched to a halt and I dove out, ready to grab everything I might need, having planned to bring the entire boot of equipment. The Guv was out too, barking orders into the radio. Doors to cover, rendezvous points, getting LAS and every possible free emergency service. (We use a lot of acronyms in the job, but LAS means the London Ambulance Service. Or the Greens... Or Bandage dispensers... Or Road Nurses. We also like a bit of banter between services).

I ran to the boot and stuffed everything I could into my large black holdall. Tape, snacks, high vis, and a water bottle. I also grabbed a load of different-sized evidence bags as well, in case the other officers needed them.

The last thing was the weapon tubes because they were going to be definitely a thing some CID suit would ask for.

The guv was ahead of me by a way now and I scurried after him, trailing the massive bag. Kind of like an overly prepared police snail.

More orders were barked and he told me to seal off this doorway and area including a dark staircase. It was a lobby straight out of your home nightmares and the stink of piss assailed my delicate nostrils.

Yummy. Hours stuck in pissville for me then.

The immortal words filled my head.

"Now who would live in a place like this?"

Well Loyd, if you look through the keyhole, you'll find a murderer.

Dark humour, I know. But in my defence, it's not wrong.

Throwing the bag down I hastily prepared my area as an old boy walked up. I must admit to not paying him much attention as I was still trying to do a good job for the boss. He asked about popping to his flat on the second floor to feed his cat and I thought nothing of it, so ushered him through.

"Please do it and come straight back down. We're probably only doing this as a precaution so it shouldn't be too long" I meant my little cordon area as normally the CID professionals would not seal off an entire building as par for the course.

Minutes later, he returned so I shook his hand because community engagement right?

Besides, he was an old man, no harm no foul.

Time then began sluggishly moving, the minute hand clunking its way around the hallway clock.

It had been an hour...

Or a day...

Or I was going to retire soon...

So boring.

My scene had been closed and moved upstairs after an initial panicked search of the area. I was now superintendent in charge of staircases. Proud day. The third floor was now a no-go area and I'd see that it stayed that way. Unless you had business up here and you'd then get dutifully signed in or out of my crime scene log.

The victim was indeed deceased, that much was certain having been taken away a while ago. It's probably not a good thing waking up in a black zip-up bag if you were just having a quick snooze. The gallows humour was purely to fight off the utter depression of cases like this, as it was bringing everyone's mood crashing down.

Crime scene guarding was also incredibly lonely too. People would often sign their names and then disappear, sometimes without even a word. Or because they were chatting about the scene itself, concluding the cause of death or something equally evidential.

No one liked anyone dying on their shift, even if it was one of the bad guys. Everyone was someone's loved one so it was awful, felt by even the hardest of souls. Even the worst drug dealer didn't deserve death as I still, through everything I've seen, strongly believe in second chances for everyone.

Reformed crims make the greatest of advocates too as their experiences are far more enlightening and scary for the early years villains. They could highlight from a level point what can and will happen at the crossroads of criminality.

'Chin up though', I thought.

Must keep a clear head and sunny outlook as neighbours were all poking their heads out, wondering what the eff had happened. Doors creaked open and when they caught my eye, slammed with a wave of 'whoops, sorry! Don't mean to pry!'

One lovely old dear had brought me my favourite though - a lovely cuppa with a crisp garibaldi. Scrumptious. I do love a boiled beverage as it can often ease a lot of tensions so you can get right down and really chat to people, nitty-gritty level conflabs. I think I'm destined for a nice safer neighbourhoods team in a few years, to get to know a ward, to find family in its people. That would be the ideal role for my style I think.

But not yet. I still enjoyed the whoosh of the blue light calls, the arrests and the feeling that I had helped or even saved someone.

Looking around, there wasn't much happening, and

the corridor was not a pleasant place. The smell of piss was lower here thankfully, less acrid as it was clear in the ground floor lobby area that was the preferred urinal of choice for the drunken ne'er-do-wells.

Time seemed to slow to a standstill. People came and went. I nodded hello to all of them. They just signed my book and went on with their business. The governor then appeared from the flat of death with a sullen look on his face. Undoubtedly looking the worse for wear due to the stench of death that was assaulting the nostrils, he walked past me and headed downstairs.

He never even signed my book.

Chapter Fifty-Two

The older man felt the coppery smell inside his nose and still to this day, hated it. It meant the worst. There were no two ways around it. The young trainee detective had already thrown up in the sink with everyone hoping to god that there was nothing evidential within that had now been completely corrupted.

'He was a good kid though,' thought Boone. He was eager to solve everything he could, taking all failed cases personally.

"I'm so sorry again inspector," said Trainee Detective Constable Jack Wright as he wiped his mouth again with the back of his hand. He then doubly wiped his hand with a cloth drawn from his trouser pocket. Boone smiled back at him and offered a Wrigley's spearmint chewing gum from his breast pocket.

"Always have a stash of these on you lad. For breath and the smell. Top tip." Jack seemed to note this down in his head, the mental checklist adding all the wise words uttered by the learned inspector. He slid the gum from its paper housing and unfurled the foil, jamming the grey rectangle into his mouth to chew the taste of vomit away. Both covering pieces were then scrunched together, and stuffed into a trouser pocket.

"So what do you see on the body Jack?" quizzed Boone, interested in Jack's thought process. He looked at him and watched as young eyes darted up and down the corpse, taking in details to be processed. Information became evidence, and visual details clicked into the categories of motive and method.

"Sir. The killer used a bladed weapon, possibly a

single-edged kitchen knife to first slice through the victim's throat, then stab both arteries. This was quick and professional, almost a singular movement. The suspect is clearly a doctor, surgeon or at worst butcher. He wanted this kill to be quick so as not to facilitate retaliation, which leads me to believe that the killer is smaller in stature and strength. This is backed up by the angles of the three wounds."

Jack stopped to draw breath but also to see if this was the correct track and what was expected. Not wanting to be wrong alongside respecting the inspector's feedback, he studied the older man's body language for clues to his success. Nervousness increased the gum's mastication.

"Good eye lad. Go on." Was all Boone allowed in the hope that the trainee wouldn't miss anything from his fact-based recitation. He wanted to give enough encouragement to push, but not to insinuate that the task was in any way complete.

Jack continued. "There is considerable blood splatter in the hallway, so the killer would be covered with cast off and spray, no way around it. Officers are searching the area but while there are some footprints, these stop after a few steps, the killer having removed his or her shoes."

The older man nodded in approval. He wasn't going to show the depth of his admiration for the keen eye of Jack as he wanted the apprentice detective to grow and flourish further. But he could not hold back the nod of approval which brought a smile in return.

"Uniforms were canvassing the building and the only possible suspects currently are a drug dealer on the floor above that has been shown as wanted, due to his flat being searched. The canvassing team smelt cannabis throughout the entire floor and when he didn't answer, they forced entry. There's also an elderly man on the floor below, seen leaving with a suitcase, but we are having trouble finding any details whatsoever on him."

Boone smiled widely and then started processing this new information. He had caught a glimpse of the older male as he walked in, but thought nothing of it at the time, wanting to get to the scene at speed. He chose to file it to be discussed with Alex on the way out. Jack was frantically scrawling in his pocketbook a collection of notes from the scene, details and information for later use. He was going to make an exceptional Detective once he passed his training and Boone was ready to push him forward for ranks ever higher. The job needed great coppers that cared, which is why he had taken Alex under his wing too for that same reason, both officers with great potential and bright futures. These officers were the vision of the Met that he hoped to leave behind. A strong collection of public servants ready to make the difference, those that would go above and beyond, and truly be London's saviours.

Hours passed and the various specialist teams came and went. Forensics took samples of everything, delicately dusting for any print amiss. Jack was canvassing the neighbours getting a variety of stories, an anthology of answers. He diligently noted everything, minute details became the puzzle pieces needed to complete the blood-stained puzzle.

Boone left the room and found Alex at the scene, handing off the crime scene log to his replacement. The young in-service officer looked tired having sat on the crime tape cordon for the entire shift. He'd been relieved to be relieved just once, so had heroically ploughed through, never complaining.

"Sir." Said Alex tiredly in greeting. "Time to go?"

Boone waved him away from his scene and beckoned him down the stairs, as the weary pair returned to their police vehicle. Each step felt heavy and thunderous, an effort to take having been on their feet for a good nine hours straight. Alex slumped into the passenger seat and they began the slow drive back to the station. Both officers were processing the images that they had seen and trying to lock them away, in a deep memory core so that the gruesome images were not a plague of recollection.

"Did you clock an old man as you were setting up the cordon Alex?" The question came out of nowhere for the young officer and also the inspector as Boone had been going over things in his subconscious.

"Yeah, there was some old guy, I let him feed his cat and then he went shopping or something. Lovely old man." Confused, the inspector asked for clarification.

"Do you mean you let him back into the scene?" He said it as a matter of fact as he was sure Alex would not have done such a thing. Once they were there at the scene, that was it, no matter the cat.

"Yes boss, he was there like a minute. Tiddles will be fine. Especially as the scene was moved upstairs shortly after."

Boone felt the colour drain from his face. His stomach sank. Worst-case scenarios began to fill his mind.

What ifs became tragedies. Mistakes lost murderers.

Chapter Fifty-Three

My mentor had gone a bit quiet all of a sudden.

What have I said? What have I done?

I started running through things in my head that happened today and there was nothing I could pinpoint. The minutiae of every breath was analysed as I replayed my day. Must be something policey in nature, so I reran the cordon shift.

I signed everyone in and out.

Cleared up my area, taking care to collect any crime scene detritus.

Didn't steal anyone's pens (Brought my own)

No members of the public got near the crime scene or saw anything in the room they shouldn't.

What the hell was it?

Surely not the old boy…? What harm was he? He wasn't from the same floor and he was just feeding his cat! Surely feline feeding wasn't the error? God, this is both pissing me off and shitting me up at the same time. An unusual collective feeling, I must add.

"Guv. Sorry, have I done something wrong? Sorry if I have, but you know nothing was intentional. So, sorry."

I looked at him awaiting an answer, feeling the puppy dog eyes come on unconsciously. I hated upsetting this man, well, anyone, but especially him. He was an icon for me. My own personal hero.

Panic was beginning to make me feel sick. I was sure I'd done something as he would normally be the calm reassuring type when I was going through one of my overthinking sessions. He would often break the never-ending cycle of mental turmoil with some random quote or an insight that focused my mind.

But now, he was stoic and almost ashen of face.

Nothing further was said until we got back to the yard. Boone got out of the car he'd so deftly parked through years of practice and entered the building, his strides storming ahead.

There was a young in-service Detective Constable there who was getting bags out of the boot of the CID car. It was a beaten-up Ford Focus which had seen a few undercover chases, its knocks and dents telling many a tale.

"Hi Jack." I said grinning, trying to calm myself down with some light humour. He stood up from the secluded confines of the boot lid and didn't seem to get the joke as the confused look on his face readily proclaimed.

"Hello." I followed up, sounding it out so his robotic brain would compute. He got that one and waved back, his arms filled with notebooks and evidence bags.

"You were on the crime scene cordon today." He stated matter of factly as he approached. Nodding, I slid my butt over to offer him a section of the car to lean on. A surprising amount got discussed leaning against pandas I've found in the mere two years I'd been a police officer. Loved it though, but not as much as old Android Jack, the robot of CID.

He lived for it. Strived to solve everything, even down to who stole the last biscuit from the skipper's secret jammie dodger stash. If you look up 'focused,' in the dictionary, there'd be an unsmiling passport photo of

Jack alongside an annotated collection of notes and references to back up the source material. He was so robotic, that he couldn't leave his body to science as Microsoft had already optioned it.

Jack stopped short of slouching against the car but stood near me as bolt upright. It reminded me of a scene showing a certain NS-5, stoically steadfast to Detective Spooner's aggressive questioning. Right before they got all murdery.

"Yup, that lovely job was mine. Ticked everyone in and out like a pro." I tried to be proud of the mundane task, but nope, couldn't. It was exceedingly boring.

"I think the scene will remain in place for a while. Our chief suspect is shown as wanted from the floor above, but there's an elderly male from the floor below whom we are having trouble finding any details whatsoever for. Doubtful to be the murder suspect though due to age and wouldn't have the power to bring down such a larger victim."

The old man.

That was it.

That was the thing I missed.

Chapter Fifty-Four

"Doubtful to be the murder suspect though due to age and wouldn't have the power to bring down such a larger victim."

As the sentence finished, TDC Wright watched the officer process the information and then leave, stomping off towards the rear door of the small police courtyard. He never said anything, just left, seemingly in deep thought.

At twenty-six, Jack Wright had been in the police his entire career, joining in his nineteenth year. He had risen through the ranks quickly, his aptitude for crime solving and detection noticed and nourished by the Criminal Investigation Department. They had snapped him up eagerly, needing new blood in their ranks, especially those that suited the long hours and heavy casework the role required.

So PC became TDC with the 'T,' of that acronym soon to become a thing of the past once Jack completed his training.

Jack filled out his five foot seven frame with an athlete's physique, due to his regimented exercise schedule. His training for distance running was the time he used to switch off, a time when he tried to not listen to his ever-turning thoughts.

He would concentrate on the steady, consistent sound of trainers on the tarmac and shoes on the pathway. It was his way of slowing the world whilst still moving fast within it. He would clock up mile after mile, bringing his mind back in speed with the world around him and not a thousand times analytically faster.

It had made him muscular but trim, almost sinewy, although you could never tell under the efficiency of the grey suit. It was off the peg, but smart, the lines of the single-breasted jacket clean and crisp.

His jet black hair was also cut to an efficient standard to show his professionalism whilst still being to the day's style. Not that he went out anywhere to show it off.

Jack was the epitome of a workaholic, never wanting to let a minute slip by that could be used in service of the public. He strove to save and was built to puzzle out the crimes of the evil doers, bringing them to a summary judicial process.

Sometimes the case would be airtight, with all the 'i's dotted and 't's crossed only to have the suspect let off with a suspended sentence. This would frustrate Jack immensely, but he would use this failure to ever focus himself, to make sure that justice was served for the victim.

He began to walk after the older police officer but he was already out of sight due to the urgency in his step.

Jack made his way through the building and up to the CID office where he moved to the rear of the room to his designated table. His early turn colleagues had already been dismissed with thanks and a late shift team was going through the handovers from the morning's work.

Jack placed the collection of notebooks on the table and began to refile the unused evidence bags into their correct receptacle.

"Watcha Jackie boy!" came a voice from the opposite side of the desk. It was Jack's arch nemesis, although the man sitting opposite did not know that just yet.

DC Mike Granger was the polar opposite of Jack, the chaos to his order, the yin to Mike's yang. Having been part of the team's furniture for ten years, he would readily spread the entire contents of his desk across Jack's, much to his ire. The clutter had become almost an ecosystem in itself, with detritus spreading like a plague into the OCD serenity across from it. Jack knew for a fact that the table boundaries were to be respected, each wooden rectangle a designated workspace. But for Mike, it was an extended, welcoming offer of more real estate.

But what really triggered Jack was the decorative plastic fish on faux wooden backing which he would nudge back over to Mike's side each day. Batteries long dead, Billy the Bass had no cause to be there, no reason for further existence.

Mike had brought it into the office years ago as he wanted it to be the team's mascot for some ungodly reason. When life had died in the thing after a few days, so had all hope for DC Bass joining the team. 'Small mercies,' thought Jack.

The various notebooks and paperwork were straightened on his desk and he sat, ready to read through them again in the hope that a suspect would appear in the details.

'No stone would be left unchecked,' he mused.

Chapter Fifty-Five

The kettle began to splutter into life as the water inside grew in temperature. It had been a long day for everyone and Boone thought back on the day's incident. Every angle had been covered and all information gathered. He was happy to have Wright in CID because he would pick up on all things left unfurled by all other officers.

He was also glad to have Alex along for the ride today as well, but the elderly escapee was troubling him.

Had they let the killer walk away?

Had our prejudgements on his age and appearance let a killer walk free?

He sure to hell hoped not. It probably would end up in a drug dealer's dispute as there were grinders and scales within the victim's flat. There was also a litany of the small plastic sealable baggies used by cannabis sellers to have the correct weights in amounts ready to go for rapid transactions. The victim had previous for both selling and carrying, but the Possession With Intent To Supply had never stuck on the large deceased male.

Not that it mattered to him now. A wry smile crossed the inspector's face, aware of the darkness of the humour. For many officers, it was a coping mechanism as the things they often saw were scarred in memories. People treated others with contempt worse than a layperson could ever imagine and Boone had seen his fair share.

Christ, he hoped it was as simple as a drug deal gone bad.

He had visions early that the old man had somehow

pulled off the murder for whatever reason and then we'd let him wander off. He could see the headlines now and it made him shudder. That rag which defined itself as a newspaper, the 'News of the World,' would have a field day dragging the entire police force through the mire.

Boone hoped that some irked celebrity scandal would end the news (in highly inverted commas) paper and it would close, never to darken a paperboy's satchel again. Police were always tarnished with the same brush for anything everyone ever did anywhere which was a constant annoyance. Boone wished the good work his troops did daily had the same effect.

He sighed as the kettle clicked off its completion and the door flew open.

Boone looked up annoyedly at PC Alex Chambers, his ward and protégé.

"Sorry boss." The constable took a step back, closing the door slightly. He knocked whilst still being in the room, more as a mark of respect than an option to enter.

Boone waved his hand as entrance acceptance, digging around the office for a clean mug. Alex always took a cup of tea when offered to the point the inspector knew how he took it without asking. The office was a multi-use one, shared by a variety of local inspectors, some more respectful of mug etiquette than others.

Boone sniffed at one and recoiled, throwing it directly into the bin as no scrubbing was going to save that receptacle. He picked another, noticing that it had the 'thin blue line,' flag on it.

The white mug was emblazoned with the black and blue logo in quite a stark contrast to each other. He knew the original meaning, that of 'embodiment of the unbreakable component of law enforcement standing as a safety barrier between the law-abiding citizens and the criminally inclined'. It stemmed from a quote from the fortieth president of the United States of America, Ronald Reagan who once said, "Evil is powerless if the good are unafraid." From there on, history spread the flag throughout law enforcement.

But nowadays, it seemed to represent the dwindling numbers of officers, 'the ever-thinning line we hold', he thought.

Dropping the off-brand tea bag into each of the mugs, he filled both vessels with boiling water. Topping off with milk and sugar, he stirred, still in silence, lost in thought.

Alex took one from the table as Boone's thoughts drifted through the day's action, snapping the inspector back into the same reality.

"Guv, there was an old man, he wanted to feed his cat. I let him through the cordon I was setting up. He's not connected, is he? Please say he isn't. Oh God, he is, isn't he? What have I done...?" Alex was going through a string of emotions, his overthinking nature running rampant. Boone placed a hand on his shoulder reassuringly.

"I don't think so, lad. The victim was pretty sliced up. They think it was a drug deal gone wrong as there was a known dealer living upstairs. He's suspect number one right now and uniforms are on the lookout."

Boone felt that he was almost convincing himself at the same time knowing that, albeit slim, the old man could be a suspect.

A suspect they had let walk away from the scene of

the crime.

But wasn't he leaving when they got there?

Why go back to the scene of the crime when you were basically scot-free and clear?

Boone decided that he wasn't the suspect after all, as why to God would you risk getting caught? There was literally no good reason.

At that moment, he decided that he would not need to mention Alex's failure to anyone.

No one needed to know...

Chapter Fifty-Six

The kettle clicked again having been boiled twice previously. The exasperated clack of the off switch seemed to be getting more and more annoyed with each unused boil. It simmered its anger down to mere steam as the heat began its subsidence.

Jack was staring out of the first-floor window at the lights of Kingston Town Centre as the window was clouded by the kettle's fuming. They blurred in and out of focus as his mind drifted over details within, his mental checklist analysing each evidential minute of the day. Lost in thoughts, he clicked the kettle to boil once more.

Sat in the police station, he knew it was located away from the main shopping lanes, but close enough to hear music and laughter from the nearby pubs and eateries. Not that he cared for either right now. He was plagued by information received, something amiss with details unlinked.

The kettle clicked off again, this time quicker than before due to the previous boils. It tooted out a blast of steam in frustration, settling back into a heated anger.

As Jack moved papers back and forth, twisting and turning photos to get a better understanding of events unseen, a large globule of ketchup splattered onto an injury depiction.

"Oh. That's ironic isn't it?" Mike chuckled through a mouthful of burger. "It's like sauce on your crime scene photographs. One for Alanis Morrisette there!" He guffawed, spraying further mouth contents onto Jack's desk as he leaned over the organised harmony.

"Mike! This is evidence! Go away!" Jack replied irritably. He began brushing away the larger errant morsels with a tissue from the Kleenex box he kept to the left of his second drawer. He also kept an array of other cleaning materials within, so that his desk remained prestigiously clean. He delicately cleaned away all the escaping detritus until his desk was returned to order, except for the pandemonium that was DC Mike Granger, who had taken up a perch on the end.

Mike shifted Jack's paperwork into a cluttered pile, plonking his ample behind on the corner, raising both feet to a nearby chair.

Everything about this movement was unacceptable to the younger trainee Detective. There's a chair - sit in it. Desks are for organised paperwork, not piles of clutter or arses.

'Arses in all meanings of the word,' Jack thought angrily, staring as the older man shoved the remnants of the burger into his gaping maw. He had to poke all of the destroyed burger further in with a pudgy digit, removing it quickly before the mastication process began. Jack noticed that the finger was covered in sauce and grease and winced as Mike picked up a photo, smudging the mess over the rear of the image. It left a smear of turmoil against the calm serenity the sheer white photo's backing once possessed. It was the definition of the officer's relationship.

"If there was a time to go postal..." Jack said unconsciously out loud.

"What mate?" Replied Mike.

Realising his unexpected omission, Jack batted it

away, hoping the detective wasn't as Sherlock as he hoped. Emotions were returned to normal, frustrations were however not.

"What do you think happened?" Although he cared not what he thought, his summation was irrelevant to the facts of the case. Many officers went with instincts and to Jack, 'gut feelings,' played no part in solving crimes, just evidence. Numbers, statistics, and information were the facts that held up in court, but Jack just needed the topic changed, from his earlier spontaneous outburst.

So Mike's opinion, he would stomach.

"Drug deal gone wrong. The geezer upstairs did it. All these drug dealing wankers are all the same. They'd all stick each other if it got them an extra pony." Jack wondered what the equestrian link was to drug dealers, whilst musing on most of the content of what Mike had muttered.

He hated colloquialisms, opting for statements of the obvious. Words were often wasted on the intellectually challenged members of society, so he wanted to not waste any on anyone. Jack suddenly realised that conversations were supposed to be two ways and Mike was looking at him for his turn to reply.

"Hmmmmm" was all he could muster, alongside an obligatory head nod and chin hold.

"Case closed then. Go home. Didn't you finish two hours ago anyway? Go home to your bird." Again, another wildlife reference. Surmising that he must have meant 'cat,' as he did indeed actually have one of those, he remembered that he needed to buy her food on the way home. There would be feline hell to pay if he didn't...

The young animal had been brought for him by his sister, Sarah. She had thought he needed company within the walls of the solitary flat, which should be filled by a kitten of all things. He'd been told to give her a name as well, something Sarah took great pleasure in. She knew it would make Jack squirm as imagination was almost an alien concept to his analytical thought process. He'd opted, after much consternation for 'cat'.

Mike sauntered off to chat with another officer who had entered CID's walls. Jack watched as the pair chatted and guffawed, taking the chance to return his attention to the now chaotic clutter of evidence.

There was something he was missing.

Evidence yet to be found.

Chapter Fifty-Seven

His life story would make a hell of a television series. He'd begun life as Tom, then fled to Oliver, lastly to Gerald but with each name amendment, more torment was brought.

Ever since he was a child, the urge to inflict pain was a curiosity he'd tried to keep hidden from the world. Starting on small animals and then lashing out at his younger sister, his fascination for inflicting pain was a darkness best kept hidden. In those brief moments that he allowed his inquisitive depravity to take control, someone suffered.

So more for his own sake, he kept it hidden.

But then one night, the awakening happened.

Tom had seen his blood coursing from his arm and wished to retaliate, feelings of hate boiling within. He was forced to the floor, scared out of his mind as his inner malevolence clawed to the forefront. It scratched its way to the surface as it had done before, but Tom had been in total control at those points. Now, it was taking all his strength to stay in charge of his actions.

This was the night he failed in that task.

Going to his parent's room, he saw that his father had brutally murdered both his mother and sister. The snap in his mind was an almost audible crunch to Tom and the small boy that he was, died that night.

Control was now lost for Tom, and he became a mere audience to his actions, as he handed over governance to his innermost maliciousness.

And retaliate he did.

The blooded knife felt delicious in his grasp and sliding it into his father felt just exquisite. Whilst non-sexual in nature, the sensations were similar, and rippled though every fibre. Death was a conquest that brought sensations to his body, tingling through his entire nervous system.

This pleasure would return many times throughout his life at differing levels but was most exquisite with Helen. This was his riskiest kill, but as such, the sweetest. A thrill tinged with a lovely hint of vengeance.

He never had intended to kill her at any point though. Oliver was born into the life she wanted, as subservience was a perfect cover. No one would ever suspect this mouse of a man. But Tom risked raising his head, wanting the parental love he had lost all those years before. It had been a mistake, causing the small boy to be forever banished into the mind's depths, to hide forever in the dark abyss.

Oliver then had to disappear, because he was a killer now also. And Gerald was born to be the ultimate shadow.

But hiding from the police became both tiresome and time-consuming though. He had wanted a base of operations, a home to continue his unending needs and desires.

But Helen had ruined that. The bitch.

She was his first trophy to compensate for Oliver's loss. He kept it in a lock box which was just big enough to hold her heart that he had butchered out of her chest cavity whilst she was still alive. Once free, the organ took up permanent residence in a glass jar, filled with water, never to be opened again.

From there, he burned the Oliver persona, disappearing once more.

Gerald then took cash-in-hand jobs and hid himself even further. No friends, not even work acquaintances were allowed close. He hid his presence in the world doing tedious manual labour, and often left him too tired for his urgent passion.

This newly created name of Gerald Heggarty was consistent and he remained it to this year, 2009. It had served him well, a person on paper alone. Wealth was hidden from previous lives, some stolen from victims, and he eked out a meagre existence. He wanted for nothing but the next morbid high, coming up with creative accidents for unknowing victims.

Nothing felt the same since Helen though. The feeling of his hands inside her chest cavity was beyond anything he'd dreamed of.

He longed for it again and it was a crushing weight.

The voice in his head began around this time and as he was in his late sixties, he initially ignored, but it grew louder, pushing his behaviour, and confusing his senses. He began to lose time, waking in places he knew not, so he took to locking himself away in the small flat, his only human interaction was with the food delivery person that changed weekly.

The voice seemed to be born from fragments of his broken mind, taking on the characteristics of the people he'd killed. Parts were his father, others the screams of victims nameless. All were a jumble though, easily quashed when Gerald set his mind to the task.

Helen became the loudest voice amongst them, possibly because of their past connection. She seemed to want vengeance, trying to get him to make mistakes so he would get caught at best, and killed in retaliation at worst.

'It wasn't her though,' Gerald reasoned. Couldn't be. She was very much dead.

This year was the closest of calls as he never meant to kill the man upstairs, never intended to 'shit on his doorstep,' as the saying went.

The Helen trick his mind played had killed him and he was almost caught, had he not realised what her plan was. He was lucky that the police officer had a kind heart that he had taken full advantage of.

Luckily he still had his lockbox with his treasure concealed inside.

Its beat long forgotten.

Chapter Fifty-Eight

Control was within her grasp.

She could feel it.

Her awareness had dawned sometime in the years after her death, however, an unknown amount of time had passed. Within her ethereal state, it was hard to judge time's normal passage.

It had taken longer still to come to terms with her situation.

She had become bodiless, a ghost in the mind of her killer. Within those dark recesses, she began to realise the man she once thought to take financial control of, was a much more secretive, maleficent beast.

She'd found other voices too, all screaming incoherently at each other, all feeling the pain of their deaths still, even lost in this dark void.

It scared her to the core of who she now was. Who, or what, she had become. She didn't understand how either, just knew she had somehow gripped onto life and was holding on somehow.

She tried to hide from the disjointed pain, but the constant screams of the murdered rang out insistently through the inky blackness.

There was no respite from the tormented hell she was trapped in.

Years seemed to pass. The screams only grew as more voices joined the thronged mass. None became as clear as hers though. She could pick out male or female from the sound, but there was no personality to any of them.

Except for the one man.

He existed in the darkest corner of the mental prison. He never said anything, just remained there, unaffected by the wails of the dead. Without form, he still seemed to stare off into the distance, surrounded by a crippling sadness. It was a hollow bleakness away from the screeching chaos and for Helen, her only respite. She would exist there from time to time as the sheer loneliness gave her time to plan and plot her next move.

In this barren plain, she could almost see the world around her, through the eyes of her captor. She would watch his movements, see and feel his kills. Every time he murdered someone, strangers mostly, she knew another voice would join the screaming chorus.

And with each new inmate, she, they, felt that they were losing what passed for humanity.

She had to stop him. Not just for others.

But for her own brutal vengeance.

She would find a way out of hell.

Chapter Fifty-Nine

The warmth of the care home had settled me somewhat. I think I was drifting in and out of sleep, even awareness. Lost in thoughts I now couldn't remember.

The events, no, incidents of days past had had a major effect on me. More so than I thought. I'd seen death before, but normally, the person was already dead when I got to the scene. I don't think I'd ever seen anyone actually killed, and especially nothing as near brutal as Danny's death. His murder.

I needed to stop thinking of him, at least for now. Bringing myself back into reality and realising I had missed Gerald's story, I thought I heard him mention my name for a second.

"Sorry, Gerald. Did you say my name there?" The metaphorical snap back into the present moment needed confirmation. I was sure that the old boy had named me just then.

Added his hero into one of his tales maybe? I had been lost in thought through most of his narration, missing the gist entirely. It must've been good because he was still staring at me as if waiting for a response. His face was the same expressionless stoicism for the most part that I could pick out, but he looked more angry this time. Sneering almost.

I was in no mood to critique his prose. So opted for a standard thumbs-up of approval.

He'd stopped speaking and had gone back into 'Gerald land', which contained the fun-filled roller coaster where he sat staring out the window most days and very little happened. He was probably concocting a new novella for me and the next one I promised myself I would not miss.

I was still stuck on everything that had happened over the last few weeks. I don't think I can be blamed for it loitering in my thoughts and memories, to be honest. These were the kinds of things normal people barely saw and didn't have to deal with. They just carried on with standard life things whilst the emergency services dealt with things they only saw in the make-believe world of Saturday night telly.

"Maybe I should take some time off?" I said to Gerald on a tangent, though not expecting an answer, let alone a supportive discussion. I had initially intended on going back to work tomorrow, as I was renowned for carrying the world's weight on my shoulders. Claire would often try to shoulder some of this burden and in my defence, sometimes I had tried to let her. But when I would recount the day's work to her, I could see the effect on her face.

I took to just withholding details and receiving a supportive shoulder or a warm hug that lasted too long. She would know then that it had been a rough one, words and details left unsaid.

I stood up and gave the elderly codger a couple of reassuring taps on the shoulder.

"No..." The word was a rasping, gravelly tone, dragged forth from some deep hole. The whispered voice gave me the immediate chills and I turned around to respond to the female voice.

No one was around.

No one could have muttered a single word.

I resigned myself to the knowledge that I was indeed losing it and was suddenly glad Jess had signed me off. It was handy as my lost marbles really needed locating.

Walking away from Gerald, I decided to take some 'me time,' and get my butt home. I needed to be out of there, quickening my steps as I went. I turned to wave at Gerald but he didn't respond, just sat there. As he does.

Each step I took away from him brought me closer to home, or Claire as I like to call her.

The walk home felt like an age, and I often quickened my pace, wanting to be nearer to Claire. She could and would help. All this pain would be shared and I'd melt into her embrace.

As I opened the door, I heard her footsteps approach. And as our eyes met, the cliché became a reality.

Without words, she grabbed hold of me and I cried.

*

Neither of the pair felt or saw the dark presence enter the house.

They became the watched, targets of the tormented soul now in their marital home.

The evil eyes looked down upon them from the shadows.

Neither of them could expect what was to come later that night, as their world was about to come crashing down.

This was the end.

The price to be paid.

Chapter Sixty

The embrace would last as long as Alex needed, Claire told herself as she stood there, holding the man she loved. He didn't have to say anything, she knew what had been all over the news, the tiniest of morsels allowed into the public media sphere by the Met's press office.

Many of the staff there wanted to scream all the details out about what the officers faced, sometimes daily in the busier of boroughs, but were bound by the sub judice of media law, ever fearful of ruining incoming court cases.

Claire knew that in all of the police stories that were released publicly most of the details would have to wait until after the incident had gone to court, And in today's social media-obsessed world, would be lost on the thirty-second reel memory span of the user.

She hated social media. They had banned the online channels in their home opting for more, ironically, social mediums. Most nights they would sit snuggled on the sofa watching television together, or if Alex wanted to watch his true crime shows, she'd opt for a book, albeit still nestled in each other's ergonomic embrace.

The thought of the two together made Claire idly stroke Alex's head, bringing a wave of strength to his arms which were encircling her waist. It showed her an unconscious 'thank you,' for her comforting gesture.

In the dimly lit hallway, where shadows danced with the weight of his sorrow, the loving wife enveloped her sad husband in a warm, reassuring hug. As their bodies pressed together, it was as if the world outside had ceased to exist, if just for that moment at least. The silent strength of her embrace conveyed more comfort and understanding than any words could muster. Her arms held him securely, like a sanctuary against the storm of his emotions. In that tender moment, his tears found solace on her shoulder, and the depths of his sadness were met with the boundless love flowing from Claire, promising that they would weather this emotional tempest together.

Neither knew how long passed, both were lost in the moment, but it was broken by the electronic alert from Claire's computer. She had a team meeting planned so shipped off Alex for a relaxing bath where the water's heat would replace her warm embrace.

He agreed and started upstairs, heavier-footed than normal.

As she sat down at the makeshift desk, she heard the slosh of water beginning to fill the bath.

*

Alex lay in the water for what seemed to him like hours, as he watched the soapy bubble mountains pop and disappear randomly. Occasionally he would idly pick up a handful of the delicate soapy froth and duck it under the water, destroying the collected mound in his grasp.

They continued to gradually disappear, leaving the water as empty as his thoughts, and as the light of the sun began to diminish, it brought a cool darkness to the room.

*

Claire was busying herself with dinner when Alex reappeared. Her team meeting had been cancelled before it even started, so she had taken that time to prepare a roast for them both, and the lustrous smells brought Alex downstairs like the cartoon mouse following the enticing cheese smell. She'd roasted a chicken from the freezer and it was that which he wanted to most. They ate, watching one of Alex's shows together. This one was about a killer in the fifties and a missing child. As they watched, the hair on the back of her neck rose as her subconscious processed the image on screen.

The narrator was describing the family home of the Gardeners in Wandsworth. They had had a happy life when someone had killed both parents with a knife and suffocated the young daughter. There were no signs of a break-in and the mystery had deepened when it was revealed that the young son went missing, never to be seen again. The only evidence he existed at all was his blood on the kitchen table.

Claire's mind was racing. It was analysing the details coming in, and sending waves of chills down her back to warn her of the incoming conclusion. She looked at Alex who was eating everything with a vigour born of hunger. He was paying no heed to the cold case being outlined in great detail, his attention on the food instead.

She suddenly snatched up the remote to pause the show mid-flow. Her plate of half-eaten dinner crashed to the floor as she bolted to her feet.

The story being outlined was Gerald's first tale.

The old man wasn't making it up.

He was the young boy.

Gerald was Tom Gardener.

Chapter Sixty-One

The darkness in the room shifted and oozed. Shadows undulated unseen as they writhed and merged. The blackness of the shadows stayed a constant to the naked eye, but it had a life to it, and it was waiting.

Within the dimly lit room, a malevolent shadow seemed to defy the laws of physics, manifesting itself as an eerie, shape-shifting presence. It clung to the corners like a sinister spectre, its tendrils stretching ominously whilst unseen. This wicked obscurity exuded an unsettling aura, casting an oppressive shroud within the front room. But it went unnoticed as the flickering of the television kept the pair's attention.

The formless Helen amalgam looked down upon the pair in the room with a hateful vision. It was a mix of jealousy and rage, vengeance and longing.

She knew what had to be done.

She would do it tonight.

The grouped masses did not want to kill Claire as she was innocent, but the years inside of Gerald had twisted the dead's morality to match the violence of the host.

Claire must be sacrificed so that Alex would be forever crushed, his love murdered in front of him. He would feel the pain of loss as so many of Gerald's victims had before this evening. He was the cause of further deaths inflicted on families after his gesture allowed Gerald the freedom to do so. He had also missed the chance to bring the serial killer to justice, to make the families whole once again, vindicated by justice.

Everyone in this sorry tale now would be punished.

The voices in Gerald's mind had given her strength and she had learned from them, grown within them. They had found the hidden persona of Tom, the small boy trapped alongside the collected dead, whom Gerald had begun life as. After trauma on trauma, he'd been reborn after killing his father into the man Helen had married.

The man who had mutilated her.

Torn her apart.

A violation that required vengeance.

She had then grown into this spiritual essence that could affect the waking world. The voices were a torrent of screams at the beginning, one by one absorbed, giving her a more consistent darkness. The many voices in his head were from all the victim's past, and they allowed her time outside of the mental prison. In agreeance with the amalgam, she started trying to stop Gerald. But he continued hiding behind the guise of dementia, poorly diagnosed by an overworked doctor. The voices had changed Helen's spirit persona, which had started out trying to get justice for the murdered, into a vengeful, hate filled entity of righteous fury, intent on killing, or even destroying everyone that was allowing Gerald to continue.

Consciously or unconsciously. This is why Claire needed to die, to break Alex. His death would come near to the end when he was a shell of a man. Because he had missed the best chance to capture Gerald, he would feel the pain.

He would be there at Gerald's end, and he would be the one to find Helen's heart.

Chapter Sixty-Two

The realisation held her for moments, stuck in the gut-wrenching truth of it all. Her stomach felt as if it had dipped like going down, then suddenly lurching upward again on an old country lane.

Thoughts were rushing through her head and took the form of a jigsaw puzzle as the pieces slotted together effortlessly.

The old man Gerald wasn't telling Alex a story, he was confessing his past. That of Tom Gardener in Wandsworth in the fifties.

Another wave of nausea hit her.

The second story.

She tried to recall details.

What was the murdered woman's name again?

Closing her eyes, she tried to remember any details that would help her.

Harriet?

No, that wasn't it.

Helen.

Helen's heart. 'Oh God, that poor woman,' Claire said aloud.

She needed to know if this one was also some sort of cold case repeat. The series Alex watched had hundreds of episodes, all dealing with some horrific event.

The one now playing was dealing with a trainee police detective sergeant called Wright who had been set upon by some sort of dog unleashed by an unknown owner.

The skipper was being played by an attractive male lead in fairness, but that was irrelevant at the minute.

She grabbed the sky remote from her husband and began searching for each episode's description. More unsolved murder descriptions filled the screen as she scan read through them.

Alex was staring at her waiting for a reason for her actions and she held a finger up indicating that he should wait. The stern look of concentration was enough of an extra indication that an interruption would not be wise. He began his patient wait for answers.

Two series back, she found another dog attack episode but chose to ignore it, although found the similarities strange. Again, more terrible descriptions filled the screen, flicked away when content described something different to what she sought.

Another dog attack…

She flicked ever onwards until she swiped, stopped and returned to the one in series seven.

Helen.

She had found her. The episode described how her husband, Oliver, had flipped, killing her and cutting her up with some sort of home DIY tool, murdered in her living room.

She started the episode and pictures from the seventies began telling the tale of the inconspicuous family. 'No one could have thought what happened could ever happen…,' came the ominous tone foretelling the horrendous incoming outcome. As the details unfurled, the narration began to fill the pit of her stomach with dread.

Alex was also now transfixed with the story, having realised the same as Claire. He was showing a mixture of shock and horror alongside utter confusion as the person whom he had been conversing with had been a killer.

Claire was the first to speak, her voice initially breaking before a cough levelled it off to some form of normalcy.

"Alex... It's Gerald. Oliver is Gerald... and Tom. He was in the episode from earlier. He's telling you his life story. Oh God."

The incredulity was strident in the last few syllables.

"Has he told you another story?" Claire wanted to know.

The colour ran from his face as his subconscious brought back enough details from the most recent tale to link to his memories.

Alex realised that the stories were linked through time, each a confession of things past. Gerald was confessing to his previous sins as he was now in his last moments, his dementia allowing brief glimmers of the past to escape, thus easing his conscience.

Alex also came to the realisation that the person he had been talking to was the old man from the crime scene which was such a defining moment in his career and notably his life.

He looked from the television back to Claire, and as he did, his vision focused on the shadowed movement behind her.

Chapter Sixty-Three

As the conversation and more so the realisation were pieced together like a horrific jigsaw, Helen knew it was time. She watched Alex's face collapse as stories became reality.

Fiction became fact.

She had allowed the pair to realise, but also to remember. The All wanted the officer to conclude on his own as that would add to the pain, making it so much sweeter.

As she had grown in her spiritual awareness, her initial plan of justice became a twisted form of malicious vengeance as more and more voices joined her. Seeing a means to play out their various retributions, their pain twisted her into the voice of the many. She became an amalgam of hate, a venomous fusion of loathing, and with each new persona that joined them, the strength of feelings only grew in power.

All the living who were part of this story would feel the utter devastation their collected deaths had brought.

They vowed vengeance for abrupt ends.

They promised pain for the heartbreaking betrayal of the wife.

They wanted justice for her mutilations endured.

The All were anger incarnated.

Moving from their shadowed hiding place, they swept into the room behind Claire. Whilst this woman was innocent, this would please one of the many voices whilst also hurting the police officer. They all allowed the murderous presence of John Gardener to form, to take the lead in this culling.

It moved to the forefront and became a forceful entity within the masses. As it thrust its way through, it was a choking grasp on the rest, like crushing hands clawing their way up to an ethereal form. He wanted to take this kill and they would let him.

The burning desire for revenge can be an all-consuming and deeply emotional force. It had festered within John since seeing his wife's torrid affair play out. It was a smouldering ember in his soul, driving him to seek retribution against anyone in love. His thirst for revenge felt overpowering to The All, an unrelenting need to balance the scales of justice and reclaim a sense of power that was taken away.

They knew it was futile but it consumed his thoughts, dictating his actions and decisions, leading him down this path in a desperate attempt to garner any short-term satisfaction.

It was a bitter taste to everyone, but his heightened emotional state was the destructive force they required. This would be a twisted vengeance for his own wife's dishonesty. Helen felt the pain of John's heart, and mind, breaking so had no strength to stop him. But secretly, she wanted it too.

The shadowed mass grabbed Claire from behind, easily lifting her from the chair. A dinner plate crashed against the wall as a flailed kick lashed out. Her hands grasped at the indistinct grip around her neck as breathing became almost impossible. She had been lifted off her feet and was now being held against a wall, feet thrashing below her, trying to find anything to stand on. Claire's mind reasoned that she was somehow being hung, so in desperation tried to ease the weight on her neck.

Almost immediately Alex was on his feet, rushing to her side. He too was trying to make sense of the situation as he could not fathom what was causing it. With one arm, he hooked it behind Claire, trying to lift her, whilst also trying to relieve pressure on her neck that they were now both grasping at.

He looked up at her. There was a shadow there that was caused by no normal light source and it moved as if it had a life behind it. It was what was holding her and now becoming clearer, more solid in state. The details of a male's hand formed, but entirely jet black, not one from any Earthly skin tone he'd ever seen. He felt the adumbral grip's malice but could not touch it.

Looking around in sheer panic now, he noticed another form taking shape from the inky blackness.

The expressionless face of Tom Gardener oozed out of the shadow.

The lifting of Claire brought some respite to her and she gulped down a lungful of air, buying scant moments of oxygen before the grip seemed to tighten once more. The shadow had no earthly muscles, so Alex could not be sure where the strength was coming from.

Claire's eyes bulged and she began losing colour in her face as the constraint tightened.

The shadow mass brought more human features to its form and a female face joined the males. It was below and to the left, almost subservient to the male's appearance. Her emotion shown was anger, alongside despair which brought an underlying sadness to her features.

"We want you to know what you've done. You let the host go, Alex."

The voice was a mix of masculine and feminine, rasped out from nowhere indefinable as neither of the mouths moved, their expressions constant. The sound had an echo to it, like multiple versions of the same sentence being repeated out of sync.

"You made all this happen. Their deaths are on you."

Again neither of the faces mouthed the words and Alex was struggling to comprehend the situation whilst trying desperately to help Claire. She was managing to gulp the occasional lungful of air but through the hand's dark translucency, Alex could almost see the reddening of Claire's neck where the ethereal fingers dug in.

"Please leave her alone, she's done nothing wrong!" Alex pleaded, his words breaking.

"Come and talk to Gerald, Alex. There you'll find Claire's murderer." The sentence was pleasure filled and triumphant, but as the words became intention, Alex shrieked, panicking.

Claire managed to look down at the man she loved, tears streaming from her eyes as her neck was crushed under the weight of an ethereal grip.

Multiple audible cracks were strident in the room and her head immediately lolled to one side, incapable of holding the weight of her head. Claire's neck imploded in on itself as the grip crushed inwards, bringing death almost instantly.

She hung limp instantly, all further fighting an impossibility.

And then the shadow was gone.

All that remained was a broken man and the anguished scream of loss.

Claire was gone.

Chapter Sixty-Four

In the years since his first meeting with PC Alex Chambers, Jack had barely crossed paths with him. The occasional meeting in the corridor was always greeted with a smile from the older officer and a nod of approval from the younger detective. When Jack's career progressed through the ranks to trainee detective, to substantive DC, then Sergeant and now in training for the inspector rank, no one expected anything less. He was highly decorated in duty and while not wholly liked, was appreciated by staff as a skipper that got things done.

He had always been diligent with his caseloads, making sure that his team had enough to be busy, but not enough to be stressed, so often kept cases for himself to assist.

He had taken on the murder of PC Danny Morgan himself alongside the obligatory referral to the Independent Office for Police Conduct. Whilst said reference was standard practice, Jack wanted to look into all officer deaths. It was a matter of principle for him, especially if the IOPC's report came back with inadequacies.

'The death of all officers must be treated with the utmost respect and given the appropriate due diligence,' Jack reported to himself.

This case though was not for the faint-hearted. Alex was front and centre to the murder, his Body Worn Video capturing the complete story. Jack knew from that alone that there was nothing that Alex, or anyone could have done to stop the horrendous murder.

One thing was sticking with Jack though. Redburn's

final words. They seemed to be incorrect to the DS, a mystery that did not compute in his logical mind.

"She won't get me..."

There was no 'she,' in any of the officers,' BWV. Not even a customer.

Was there someone they had missed?

Was she the cause of this tragedy?

The report had been fully dealt with and the definition of open and shut as both victim and murderer were deceased. But the female characterisation stood out to Jack.

Why?

All body-worn cameras of the attending officers had been meticulously picked through. Each frame analysed and checked by DC...

An issue arose, and Jack felt an internal twinge from an injury received from a particular personal case a couple of years ago. He'd been wounded whilst dealing with a violent suspect who did not want his large aggressive dog taken away from him. It always flared at times of heightened emotions and Jack rubbed at it to try and stem the feeling.

He returned his attention to the body worn video, but kept his hand still at the long healed wound sight more as comfort than medicinal need.

They'd been checked by a colleague on a different team. DC Mike Granger was nearing retirement having never really amounted to anything more than a slobbering paperweight in the office. As good as medically retired a few years ago, he was normally assigned admin work by his occupational health liaison.

Jack looked over at the old officer and caught sight of his old desk, one that brought back memories of cases closed, a history he was proud of. He knew that people had been helped and saved in some cases, which made Jack feel a warmth brought by pride in his work and the reassurance brought to others.

Mike was sitting there, eating as usual. Whatever passed for lunch was being shovelled into his mouth, and great pudgy digits pushed more into the cavernous hole.

"Evening Jack." Came a mouth-filled response.

"Sergeant." Jack reminded.

"No need to be formal! You can call me Mike." The large man chortled and a lump of masticated food flew out of his mouth.

"You're not a sergeant. I am a sergeant." DS Wright confirmed. "You were tasked with going through the BWV in the Morgan murder. Did you go through Alex's as well as Danny's?"

Jack wanted to know, but could already formulate an answer. It was going to be something along the lines of 'open and shut,' or 'what's that going to show?'

"What's the point in looking at his Sergeant?" The last word carried a weight of sarcasm along with it.

Jack turned and walked back to his desk and told Mike that he would be checking through it, and all his work around this case.

Mike muttered something unintelligible, and the DS thought to turn and ask what he had said but realised that it would be nothing of either pointless or inconsequential.

Jack settled into his seat and pulled a bottle of sparkling water from his satchel. He knew it was an extravagance but he needed the treat as the incoming images were going to upset his normal stoic exterior.

He spent the next few hours checking through Mike's work, luckily not finding anything majorly wrong except the shoddiness of the handwriting.

Danny's BWV was next.

It played out the evidence that had been gathered as expected, the horrendous events as documented.

It was Danny's viewpoint of Alex that confused the situation though. In a few frames, obscured by the sunlight, was a shadow. This darkness had no place there as the store was brightly lit in all frames, but it was there.

The image seemed to be best seen in reflection from mirrored surfaces, or off Alex's centre. It was around him in all frames, almost impossible to see without the technology at hand. But frame by frame, millisecond by millisecond, Jack built up the image of a woman's face, hidden in the chaos that unfurled.

He had found her.

But who was she?

Chapter Sixty-Five

I don't…

What had happened…?

All this was wrong.

A nightmare.

I couldn't form words, or string any sort of sentence together. This was a thing of fiction. Of movies.

My Claire.

I sobbed uncontrollably, unable to comprehend anything. She is… was my all. My reason for living. Now she's here, lifeless in my arms. The pain of loss made everything hurt. My chest ached. I was wracked by insuppressible convulsions of grief. It poured out of me.

I had lost everything.

I felt so alone and crushed by everything that had led to this already, barely holding on. And now my lifeline had been taken from me.

I wanted answers.

Vengeance.

Justice.

I needed to have a point in my life because right now, there wasn't one. I picked up the phone and called Jess. No answer. I called 999 and the operator blurted almost immediately "What service please?"

I think I said my shoulder number and that I needed help. I said that she was dead. The operator tried to talk, to help, but her voice was muffled in my ears.

I kept talking.

"Tell Jess... Send a team... Inform an inspector..."

I knew I was making no sense, but couldn't string together a cogent train of thought. I heard tapping on a keyboard on the line as the call handler was frantically typing, sending the computer-aided dispatch through top local units. I don't know why I remembered that acronym of all things. It was a CAD. I was now a CAD number.

Oh God, Claire...

I heard my sobs continue as I hung up the phone.

She was gone. Like Claire was. But why?

I needed to structure a reason for all this. What the fuck was that shadow thing. How the fucking hell was it talking and what the fuck did it mean by anything?

"Fuck!" I screamed out loud.

I tried to hold her back to life and steadied her head for her as she was struggling due to the injury. What the fuck was I talking about. This was what a desperate lunatic sounds like. Claire's head lolled to one side, and while I knew it was pointless, held it to my chest. I was going through multiple stages of grief all at once as anger rose. All my negative emotions were competing for a voice, all trying to show that they were more important than the others.

Think Alex...

Claire was talking about Gerald and his stories. Gerald was the Oliver in the cold case and in the second tale. He had killed his wife.

His wife was killed.

My wife was killed.

Gerald, Oliver or whoever the fuck he was had answers. I want the answer to this. To why I lost my Claire.

The spirit ghost had told me to go to Gerald.

A siren began to fill my ears. They wouldn't believe this shit. I am the only one here. I'd be rightly taken in for questioning and will never get to find out how that cunt Gerald is involved. They would not believe the shadow story. I'd be the main suspect as there would be fuck all evidence left by 'smoke'.

"We were sitting here eating dinner and a smoke monster killed my wife" Yup. That's exactly how that would sound. I'm in the gallows humour section of grief, which meant I was losing the plot. I brought it back to anger as I picked up Claire's lifeless form.

Laying her to rest on our sofa, I quickly threw on some clothes as the siren grew louder. I reckoned to have maybe two or three minutes to get out and run to find my answers.

I left a note on the table along with anything that could be tracked.

"Get DS Wright here. I did not do this."

Underneath that, I scrawled down the cold case episodes that mentioned Oliver and Tom, saying that both were the same person, Gerald.

I needed to get there first and have enough time with him to get the answers I sought so I left off the full address, just that he was in a local care home. Jack was a great detective, he'd find us.

Leaving the door on the latch, I ran out into the night as the blue and red lights started rounding the corner.

Chapter Sixty-Six

Jack sat staring at the screen trying desperately to make some sense of what he was seeing. He even tried to juxtapose viewpoints from different cameras but the rest were looking towards Danny and Redburn, not away.

He sat there for long moments trying to think of anything that would explain this. Everything he could think of was quickly muted though as the expressionless face came from nowhere scientifically possible.

'How often have I said to you that when you have eliminated the impossible, whatever remains, however improbable, must be the truth?' came the famous quote from Sherlock Holmes, but it was one that he cared not for. He much more preferred;

'It is my business to know what other people do not know,' which was more central to his scientific mind. There were no improbables, only facts as yet uncovered.

He was still sitting there when the call came in.

"He's a bit of a shit magnet isn't he?" called Granger to no one distinct.

"What's happened, Mike?" Jack wanted to know.

"There's an SNT neighbourhood PC who's offed his misses. Everyone's on the way now. Real shit storm after the Danny bollocks."

Something inside Jack knew who the officer mentioned was before the name was said out loud. He snatched up his coat, bag and other needed items and flew out of the office without a word.

He took the steps two at a time in his haste to get to

the backyard, hoping that the keys for any of the marked cars were still there. His late turn CID team would have the unmarked Vauxhall out already so he would take whatever's there.

The crisp night air hit him as soon as the rear door to the office crashed open. Car choice was sparse but a single Toyota Corolla was nestled near the back. It had seen many a chase in its life and had the dents to regale its stories. Tonight would add another tale as Jack checked the dashboard for the logbook and keys.

Taking a mental note of the time and mileage for adding in later, he jumped in. The rules state that any officers taking out a vehicle must fully check the vehicle for damage, lack of oil and other deficiencies so it was safe to operate, but Jack realised the urgency of his flight.

He kicked himself for flaunting the rules, as rules were key to keeping chaos and anarchy at bay, but he was spurned on by a gut feeling. He reminded himself to check that too.

The car handled the meagre traffic deftly and sped through the parting flow of vehicles. He prepared his mind for the panicked driver who would just stop wherever they were when seeing the lights and gave everything as wide a berth as possible.

This would be the link he needed.

The constant in this was Alex. He was not a suspect at this point as Jack knew that he did not have a malicious bone in his body, let alone one to kill his wife.

'Maybe the stress had broken him,' Jack reasoned, checking through the obvious first.

The red of the bus blurred past as the DS added that to a list of possibilities to be checked through. Alex had been through a lot in the last few weeks, easily enough to send anyone over the edge. But to kill his wife?

Jack didn't think so. If Alex was to break mentally, he mused that he would rather fold in on himself rather than explode and possibly hurt others. But still, one to check through though.

The Toyota screeched to a halt in front of the officer's home as a sealed note in a bag was walked to a parked car. From the activity, he deduced that Alex was not currently here as there had been no call for a custody cell. He was an officer, yes, but would still need to be arrested and cautioned if he was to be questioned.

There was a process.

"We must trust the process," Said Jack aloud.

Reading it and analysing the handwriting at the same time, he struck the mental break possibility from the list.

This was something else.

Chapter Sixty-Seven

Gerald sat staring out of the window most days. He couldn't remember first sitting down. Couldn't even remember where the window led to.

But tonight... It didn't matter.

He was free.

His condition normally left him with blanks, missing time, and thoughts long forgotten, but clarity had revealed everything to the elderly man. His thoughts crystal in appearance.

Earlier, when the light broke, he revelled in the glory of his past kills, the intense feelings flooding back to him. They gave him strength, and he would use it once more.

Leaving his room, he walked to the nurse's station where he found Melody, one of the bitch nurses. She was the only staff member on duty in the main lobby and did not hear his shuffled approach. The desk bore an assortment of wonderful options for Gerald, but he opted for the red-handled scissors due to ease of access.

He picked them up before she'd even begun turning his chair.

"Gerald! What are you doing out..." Her words were cut short as the silver blades pierced her eardrum. Even in his weaker state due to his age, he was able to bury them far enough in to kill her almost instantaneously.

She fell to the floor with a thump and Gerald smiled as he stood on the scissor handle. He steadied himself on the desk as he did, to fully drive them deeper.

It was unnecessary but filled him with waves of

tingling pleasure.

The only other person in the room was an elderly woman sitting in one of the armchairs which faced the television.

Gerald realised that he had some time now so surveyed the room for what felt like the first time.

His eyes rested on the Haywain painting and grimaced as the painted farmer reminded him of the copy that his parents had in their bedroom.

He knew it wouldn't take much to kill the old cunt, so started wheeling the tea trolley over to her. It squeaked as it approached but the woman remained still, either deaf to it, or sound asleep.

Both worked for his purposes, Gerald concluded.

Getting to her side, he realised that she was actually looking up at him, but so frail as to not be able to lift a smile in greeting.

She was also not able to stop the large metallic hot water urn from hitting her as it was pushed from the trolley. It crashed against her face with a sickening crunching sound and she too was dead after the impact.

Gerald waited to listen as the boiling water spilt out onto her, reddening the flesh to welts, some of which popped and oozed under the intense heat.

Happy with his work, and filled with a newfound strength, Gerald thought it was time to get out of both his pyjamas and this accursed care home.

Walking back to his room, he began to sing the melodious lyrics of 'Love letters in the sand,' quietly to himself.

Chapter Sixty-Eight

The run to Shady Oaks dried most of my tears. My sleeve also carried a lot of that burden. I didn't care though. The only thing keeping me from just stopping were answers. Any sort of reason as to why.

Just the why of it.

Why her?

Vengeance and justice were pointless now in my mind as neither would bring Claire back. Neither would give me closure.

What the fuck is 'closure,' anyways? Why would I want to close this door? She was, is, my all. She made me who I am today and it wasn't enough to save her. I had failed her. Failed everyone.

And now all that was left were the answers.

Gerald would tell me one of his fucking stories, his life experiences that would answer this fucking hell I was in now. Then maybe I'd talk to officers about the whole thing and hope to fucking merry hell some evidence could be found.

If none came to light, I'd be the one going to prison as the officer who killed his wife after a mental breakdown. I'd be in all the papers and every single officer would be tarnished with my brush, even though I was innocent. Or I could be destined for a padded cell or the chance of being killed by some criminal who hates cops or wife killers.

Who the fuck cares either way though. That wasn't a question. I didn't care, except for the first one. I didn't want the media dragging the fine police family through my shit.

Claire was gone.

That was that.

Some people ask 'What did they do to deserve this?' at times of crisis. Mine was letting a killer loose. I let the killer of a drug dealer free and I lose my wife. That was wrong.

And he had killed before. How many times?

He killed his wife for whatever reason, I can't remember right now, and frankly, don't care.

Hang on. What if he killed AFTER I let him go? Oh, for fuck's sake. Those deaths are my fault. I needed to know if he killed more. This thought alone brought fresh waves of pain and stopped me in my tracks. I looked up at the sky and into the inky blackness of night and wondered how many deaths were on my hands.

It all came back to answers being needed. I forced myself on into the night.

Tonight, I will get closure.

This story is over.

Chapter Sixty-Nine

Everyone was waiting, eager for this moment. It was the end times for both the collected voices and the host. A final freedom for all concerned.

The chess game that they had been playing had come to this.

The stories were told.

The truth was out.

Gerald was due justice tonight. In what form that took, none cared. If it was vengeance from the officer, they'd hopefully be free of the mental prison that encapsulated them all. If it was justice, he would rot in prison, hopefully dying in his sleep in his own piss and shit.

The amalgam was happy with either result.

They had brought him to the brink of madness, to even cause a doctor to prescribe dementia as the reason behind his silence. He had been wrong though. Gerald was still here, fighting daily with the collected mass of the dead, waiting and plotting.

Poor little Gerald. Poor little Tom.

The shared consciousness had now become one synchronous voice, with no one leading out over the rest. Helen had been the catalyst of birth, the focus for freedom, but now she and all of them were a mere memory.

They were all that was left. They were now an 'us', a collective of pain.

They heard the door open to the main reception. He was here.

Soon...

They heard him stop for mere moments and then stride towards the closed door in the small living space The All, and Gerald resided.

He was coming. Doors began opening as he searched for them. One by one he drew nearer.

The entity grew in excitement as footsteps drew closer. As did Gerald, who was now fully aware of both the amalgam and the confines of his frail body.

They stood, and they all turned to face the door. He was wearing his only suit, ready for whatever fate would befall him. It smelled musty as it had been in the case for many years, kept for an occasion.

He was planning on leaving when the amalgam returned. They had all left through the cracks in his psyche and found Gerald in his final moments, almost ready to flee.

His case was open and ready for inspection as well, its contents neatly arranged within. Each item was a part of his legacy.

The door opened and the two men locked eyes.

Chapter Seventy

"Why?" was all Alex could muster as he saw the old man standing upright for the first time. It confused him to see the man without frailty, with none of the vulnerabilities the seated man portrayed previously.

The room was well-lit and clean as if ready for a new occupant. This was further reinforced by the open suitcase on the freshly pressed bedclothes.

"Why her?" Alex asked again, this time more forcefully. Tears began to form once more at the memory of loss.

Gerald stood emotionless and slowly raised an arm so that a bony finger could point to the case. As he did, the jacket and sleeve retreated up his arm revealing the white of a scar line. The wound travelled up his arm until it disappeared under the clothing, but showed no signs of petering out.

Alex followed the movement to the case. It contained a few items of note and not the normal folded clothing you'd expect. Moving over to it, he pulled out a sealed bag. It was taped shut but the translucency of the plastic allowed a view within. Alex shifted the item inside and crusted dirt fell from the carrier bag inside. Frustrated, he tore open the outer bag and looked into the inner bag. The blood-stained pyjamas within confirmed Alex's worst fears as he knew this was from the 2009 Kingston murder case.

He dropped them unceremoniously to one side and returned his attention to the case's other contents.

The lockbox carried a weight to it and when moved, sloshed from one side to another indicating some form of liquid was hidden inside. The key to the box had been freshly taped to the top and Alex tore it free in his attempt to see the mysterious contents.

He was not prepared for what lay within and upon seeing it, he dropped it back onto the bed.

Safely nestled was a glass jar, filled to the brim with a murky fluid. Particles floated around inside as they had come free from the preserved severed heart. Alex noticed that it was secured in the box by crumpled newspapers from the seventies which were now yellowed with age.

The murder case continued to shock as Alex noticed a wooden-handled carving knife. It had once been ornately decorated with a gold leaf but that had not survived the withering of time and only a few flecks remained. The blade was rusted and heavily bloodstained too, blunted with use.

Alex dropped the knife back on the bed as the feeling of nausea grew to a vomitous expulsion. He turned as the hot liquid rose in his throat and managed to find a small dustbin in the corner to expel the thick fluid. Wiping his mouth on his sleeve he returned his view to the cases before him.

The room seemed darker now, the shadows encroaching further into the lit areas. Even though the bulb shone with the same intensity, the darkness grew.

Alex looked at the old man who continued to just stand there. His form was outlined by the wooden frame of the old window and the darkness from the outside seemed to compliment his inner demons perfectly.

Alex was drained of everything. He felt emotionless

and empty. A husk of who he used to be. All he ever wanted was to leave a positive impression on people, and to be remembered for what he left behind.

Now all that was in turmoil.

Chaos had descended on his world and destroyed it. Because of a kind mistake. He laughed a dry chuckle and Gerald remained intently staring, not seeing the joke.

Neither did Alex, but it was the last vestige of the man he was. He had recalled many stories himself of times past as a means to help and educate, even to entertain, but Gerald's were just hideous confessions of his calamity.

Both the storytellers looked at each other, not knowing what they were about to face.

Lunging forward, Alex grabbed the old man by the collar, thrusting him back against the window. It shattered but Gerald kept his feet as jagged shards of glass fell all around the pair. The crash and tinkle of the glass brought footsteps rushing down the corridor. In seconds, they would be joined by staff.

Alex kept hold of the man easily and tried to think of something, anything to say.

Neither man had any more stories to tell.

Nothing was left in either person.

Alex pushed Gerald back against the window frame and recoiled as he felt something moving under the old man's shirt. It seemed to writhe and push forward in an unnatural way causing the police officer to step back and look down.

The skin under the old white shirt was moving, taking

some new form that Alex could not comprehend.

'Was that a face??' thought Alex, horror and revulsion building within him.

Gerald plunged the knife upwards and into Alex's stomach effortlessly, tearing through the flesh and into organs inside. Both men felt the blade enter as with the rust and age's erosion it grated its way in.

Alex stumbled back a step, but kept hold of Gerald's jacket, more for support than anything at this point. He looked into the face of the man he thought was a friend and heard the words;

"It's finally over. And we are free."

It was not his voice though. The sound had emanated from his chest and was the same echoed sync-less collection of voices all repeating the same words.

With the last vestiges of Alex's strength, before it ebbed away, he lifted the old man and impaled him on the jagged glass behind him. One large piece entered Gerald just at the base of his neck and sheared through the withered skin with ease. It protruded through, the force severing every muscle until it burst through the old man's face, pinning him in place.

The blackness welcomed Alex as he passed out, collapsing on the floor. The last thing he saw was the familiar, welcoming lights of the approaching police car.

Footsteps thudded down the corridor, but Alex knew he was done.

He cared not.

Claire would be waiting.

Epilogue

There were people everywhere when I arrived. I noted that people always defaulted to their chosen specialities when a critical incident occurred. Some would choose emergency life support, others crowd control, and a few would turn to witnesses for both statements and support.

I myself would cover the investigation so that the facts spoke their evidence to me. I was the voice of justice, to give the closure needed to family and loved ones after the criminal is brought before the courts.

This was far beyond a critical incident though.

A second officer had been murdered in a matter of weeks. A good man too. His loss would be felt across the borough and wider still, to the loved ones and communities he'd touched.

He left behind a legacy of helping others and with his death, hope came that bit closer to dying.

I'm not even mincing words here.

He helped. He was a beacon.

And a light that was now extinguished.

"DS Wright! You need to see this..." A voice rang out from the crime scene that I hadn't yet set foot in. I was taking in whatever external details were offered, but that was a call that needed attention.

Deliberately I stepped in, careful to not disturb any evidence. Both bodies were still here, having not been removed for processing as yet.

The knife lay in situ as well after every life-saving

option was exhausted. They had tried, clearly they had. I could tell that by the expended detritus of blooded gloves and pressure bandages the first responders had used. It was a kitchen sink attempt to save their colleague but had unfortunately failed.

Some would say that Alex had not wanted to stay anymore as he'd seen people recover from wounds worse. I would not be one of those people and would wait for the science.

The second deceased person was an older man in his late seventies, early eighties maybe. I noted that he was not in nightwear but a suit, which for someone living in a care home seemed odd. Especially at this hour. Surely he was where he had to be at this time?

The cause of death was obvious as the large shard of glass still poked from back to front, jutting through most of the male's mouth. I noted that a few of his front teeth were missing and were strewn about on the floor having been violently torn free.

"Hi, sergeant. I was trying to lift him off this to keep the evidence when I felt something funny under his shirt. So we had a look. This is what you need to see because I can't make any... see for yourself."

The young officer lifted the unbuttoned shirt away, audibly so due to the sticky blood coating the elderly male's garments. It was a sickening noise, wet sounding, like pulling off a soaked plaster. The officer exposed the shoulder of the deceased. Underneath the blood-splattered material was the clear definition of a smiling woman's face.

It seemed to have somehow been pushed from

behind, within somehow, but a face there was. I struggled scientifically to understand what had caused this but settled on an anomaly or some form of unique body modification.

Extreme it was, but explained it could be.

Her expression was one that was at peace, and it gave me a nagging feeling that I had seen her before.

"That is an extreme type of body modification there. I have not seen anything like that before, have you?" I asked the PC, hoping he had, because this explanation was tenuous at best.

"Nothing Sarge... it's weird though, because the other ones look fresher. If an old boy got this done on purpose, you'd have to ask yourself if he had all his marbles."

Hang on.

Did he say 'other ones?'

I finished unbuttoning the old man's shirt and exposed the entirety of his chest. Covering most of the surface area were faces, pushing out from inside.

All seemed to be smiling, at peace even.

Except one.

What seemed to be the freshest modification was emotionless, deathly even, but the detail on the stretched skin of the old man was abundantly clear. An officer vomited violently in the hallway.

Somehow, in the centre of the dead man's chest was the face of Alex Chambers.

*

The shadowy realm of the forgotten, where time and

memory intertwined, was no more. The cracks had given way to the light allowing everyone to be free.

The spectral entity, once tethered to the world of the living, had endured capture through the years, an ephemeral whisper of forgotten personas. The names of the amalgamated massed dead were now for the history books or the police reports of years gone.

Some would be erased from the annals of history, their story buried beneath the flowing sands of time.

The amalgam felt itself flowing outward from the prison, away from Gerald and into the night sky. They were no longer controlling their path and were being split to go in different directions.

They had all yearned for a release, a departure from the endless cycle of restlessness and terror, of pain and anguish that kept them bound to the earthly plane.

The ghostly form had already begun to disperse, like smoke in the wind. Their ethereal presence became increasingly fragile, wisps of pale luminance flickering in the darkness. With each passing second, their visage waned, and as they drifted they slowly faded into obscurity, but were at peace.

Their business was finished.

Their plan played out.

In the final moments of its existence, they surrendered to the inexorable currents of fate, allowing themselves to unravel and scatter into the very fabric of the universe.

No longer bound by earthly woes or the chains of their past, they merged with the celestial expanse, becoming stardust, moonlight, and the breath of the universe itself.

In their final dissolution, they realised that they were not the only evil in this world.

There were others.

There were more stories that needed to be told.